TYRO

ALIEN ADOPTION AGENCY #3

TASHA BLACK

13TH STORY PRESS

Copyright © 2021 by 13th Story Press

All rights reserved. This book or any portion thereof
may not be reproduced or used in any manner whatsoever
without the express written permission of the publisher
except for the use of brief quotations in a book review.

13th Story Press

PO Box 506

Swarthmore, PA 19081

13thStoryPress@gmail.com

Cover designed by Sylvia Frost of The Book Brander

TASHA BLACK STARTER LIBRARY

Packed with steamy shifters, mischievous magic, billionaire superheroes, and plenty of HEAT, the Tasha Black Starter Library is the perfect way to dive into Tasha's unique brand of Romance with Bite!
Get your FREE books now at tashablack.com!

TYRO

1

PHOEBE

Phoebe had a secret.

She held it close to her heart as she hugged her friends goodbye, clinging to her secret, and the handle of her antique trunk, with the same white-knuckled determination.

"I don't know how I'll do this without you and Luna," she told Aurora, embracing her friend with the arm that wasn't clutching the trunk.

Aurora hugged her back, hard - she was surprisingly strong.

"What ho, ladies," a deep voice boomed out in an indecorous manner.

She turned to the source with a deliberate slowness, so as not to encourage such a familiar tone. She was greeted with a not entirely unpleasant view of the muscular, green guard who carried her newly adopted son.

"Atlas wants his mama to find her new home right away so she can give him some supper," he told her, smiling in a teasing manner that made her feel warm all over, and then angry.

Atlas.

Who would name an infant for the god who was supposed to have held up old Earth on his shoulders? The only thing that chubby baby was going to hold up was her plans for the future.

She glanced at Aurora, who up until now had always been the life of the party.

Aurora was gazing at the golden servant who held her own new child. She looked like she had seen a ghost.

"Are you going to be okay?" Phoebe heard herself ask.

It was a monumentally stupid question. Aurora was an undercover rebel leader with an intergalactic bounty on her head. Disappearing on this frontier moon would probably be the easiest thing she had ever done.

"Of course," Aurora said, turning to Phoebe with a smile. "If you get too lonely for me, just send up a flare or something. We'll get settled in and find each other again, I'm sure."

But Aurora's blue gaze went to the horizon and Phoebe saw the moon through her friend's eyes for a moment.

It was vast.

And it was unlikely they would ever see each other again.

But there wasn't really time to argue. Aurora was already heading down the hillside to board a pretty, blue wing-steed drawn coach with her baby and its golden guard.

The third adoptive mother of their little group, Luna, had disappeared into the woods a few minutes ago on the back of a moose with antlers that looked like trees.

Surely, Phoebe's own conveyance would arrive soon, so she could get started with her own new life.

Her two friends knew that Phoebe had grown up on a farm. It was clear they had their own vision of what that meant - a small farmhouse full of children in shabby clothing, a dusty plot of land out of which wizened parents had to coax a sickly crop.

But that was a long way from Phoebe's actual life.

Luna and Aurora were both from Terra-4, a planet so poor it was almost a universal joke.

The very first Terra was almost an heirloom planet, lavished with tourism dollars from Terrans all over the galaxy wanting to taste the closest thing to "old home".

But the other lower Terras were nightmarish. They had been terraformed by early methods and had none of the newer technology and resources of the later Terras because of it.

When Phoebe had mentioned life back on '12, the other two had teased her so much for being rich that she hadn't had the heart to tell them that she was from Terra 212, not Terra 12.

Life on the family camellia plantation on Terra 212 had been easy and pleasant. Phoebe had hosted tea parties and book club meetings in an elegant mansion overlooking the fields, where an army of droids harvested the fragrant blossoms under her father's gentle direction.

She made the seasonal pilgrimages to town with her father, to drink the local brew and negotiate the sale of the crop.

Otherwise, she lived a quiet, cushioned life with little excitement.

She had planned to stay on with her daddy forever. Her older brother had already married and produced the requisite two grandchildren, so there was no pressure on Phoebe to find a husband.

Phoebe pictured herself growing old in the mansion, reading the latest books, and smelling the camellias, and never answering to any man but her sweet, single father, who had raised her to be every bit as independent as he was.

But when the drought came, it brought unexpected problems.

Problems that could be so easily solved by the right marriage. And after all, the boy from the farm next door with the river running through it had always liked Phoebe.

Her father had given her a beautiful life and never asked anything of her. So when he mentioned that Cash Donovan from next door might come calling, what was she supposed to do?

Cash was attractive enough, with that shock of dark hair, devilish blue eyes, and breeches so tight they left little to the imagination. There were worse alternatives, to be sure.

It had been a whirlwind courtship.

But the night before the wedding, Phoebe's best friend Lottie had come to her window.

Lottie told her that Cash had been sleeping with the widow Jones for years, and now he was telling everyone that he was only marrying Phoebe for her land.

And though Phoebe was really only marrying Cash for his water, the whole thing was a horrifying affront.

She had packed a few bags and snuck out of the house and down the country road to town, catching a hovercraft to the nearest station and then buying a ticket for the first shuttle off-planet.

In the first-class lounge, she browsed the message board. There were advertisements for the high-end luggage sources, and plenty of reminders to luxuriate at destination hotels.

And there was one modest invitation to interview with the Alien Adoption Agency, for an opportunity to parent a child in exchange for a plot of fertile farmland.

I could be like my father, Phoebe had thought to herself. *A single parent with a beautiful farm to tend, and no one to answer to but myself and the land.*

She had sent her communication before she boarded the shuttle. And the Alien Adoption Agency had been waiting for her on the other side when she got off.

The intake process had been strange at best, but here she was.

Ready to start a new life.

"Are you ready?" the enormous green man asked her with a big, dumb grin.

The baby in his arms chuckled.

Phoebe rolled her eyes. "Sure, where's the coach?"

"There is no coach," the man replied. "We're just heading down to the lake."

She glanced at the murky water below. "That's a long walk."

"Yes," he agreed. "We'd better get moving if we want to get there before dark."

She let go of the trunk handle and indicated that he should take it.

"Atlas might be a little shy at first," the man said, walking toward her with the baby.

"That's fine," she said, turning and leading the way down the hill. "I don't intend to be too hands-on until he's older."

She supposed that it would fall on her to carry her own handbag, since the big man hadn't had the foresight to book a proper conveyance. That was fine with Phoebe. Her bag held the small camellia plant she'd smuggled onboard with her as a token of her old life. The flower was far too delicate to entrust to this brute of a porter.

When she didn't hear his footsteps behind her right away, she turned back.

He was wearing a surprised and amused expression.

"What's in here, unprocessed electrum rods?" he asked, picking up her case with a grunt as his expansive muscles rippled with the effort.

He promptly began chuckling at his own joke before she had a chance to answer.

She was relieved to see it was just a typical chauvinistic joke about a woman having heavy luggage. In truth, he had no idea how close he had come with his guess. Only what she was keeping in the trunk was far more valuable.

She headed down the hill without further comment, and the man followed this time.

The wind whipping off the lake was brisk and actually quite pleasant. Phoebe found herself admiring the green and blue landscape of the lush moon as they walked.

"The forest is beautiful, but it's very dangerous," the man pointed out. "By the way, my name is Tyro."

"What's so dangerous about the forest?" she asked, ignoring his blatant attempt at permission to call her by her first name.

"Only the normal things during the day," he said. "But at night there's a sort of cleansing - first the piranha pigs clear the surface and then the under-cats burrow up to eat anything too big for the pigs, and of course, the pigs themselves."

"Under-cats?" she echoed.

"Sort of like Terran tigers, but without fur or eyes," he said. "But don't worry, it just means you have to be really careful after dark if you're outside the town and beach area."

"I'll be living on a farm," she reminded him. "How will this impact my crops?"

"Oh, it won't," he said, grinning at her.

The baby chose that moment to let loose with a string of strange sounds and motions of his chubby hands.

"Are you excited to go live on a farm?" Tyro asked him.

And though the man's voice was so deep and loud it made Phoebe's organs reverberate, the baby was not at all frightened, and instead banged him on the head approvingly with a small arm.

"Aww, thanks, buddy," Tyro said with a satisfaction Phoebe found irritating.

"Isn't this the lake?" she asked, pointing at the rocky shore.

"Yes, we're on the other side, though," Tyro said. "Past the village."

She buttoned her lip in displeasure and walked on.

The village was small at least. Walking through it wouldn't take too long.

The stone streets were dusty, but the little houses with their terra cotta style roofing were rather charming, in a frontier homestead sort of way.

Along the main street, vendors stood under tents, offering their wares.

She scrutinized each stand as she passed, knowing that she would be doing business with some of these shop keepers one day soon. The owners with the neatest tents and best selections would be able to pay the highest price for her crops.

"Are you hungry?" Tyro offered, clearly misreading her interest in the stalls.

Her stomach chose that moment to grumble.

"Say no more," he laughed. "Now let's see, I think this will be the best one."

He pointed at one of the more modest tents.

"He hardly has anything on display," Phoebe protested.

"That means he doesn't have to advertise," Tyro told her. "Come on."

He marched into the tent, leaving her no choice but to follow.

She listened while he dickered with the shopkeeper, the two of them negotiating in a friendly way until they came to some sort of an understanding.

The man wandered into the back and came out again a few minutes later with a huge sack.

"Okay, princess, I've only got two hands," Tyro said, arching an eyebrow. "What do you want to carry? The baby, the groceries or your trunk?"

She blinked at him in unhappy surprise, then grabbed the sack.

The shopkeeper's rusty laugh cut the air.

"Come on," she said crisply to Tyro.

"Cheers," Tyro said to the shopkeeper, giving a little salute.

They headed back onto the street.

The sun had begun to dip in the sky, and only one or two other customers were walking around. Phoebe recalled reading about the significantly shorter solar cycle on Clotho. That would take some getting used to.

Despite her feelings about being put to work hauling the goods, she had to admit that the food in the sack smelled incredible. She peeked inside to see some sort of baked goods wrapped in paper and a couple of pounds of unrecognizable produce.

"There's no milk," she said.

"There are cells in the icebox, don't worry," he told her. "That was all set up for us ahead of time."

She nodded, satisfied. That made sense. Of course the

droids would have been programmed to ensure that she had a full larder. She was curious to see exactly what kind of equipment had been provided for her. She was prepared to be roughing it this far from the inner rings, which probably meant only a small contingent of older-model droids. But she had always been resourceful, and she was determined to make do.

They walked along in peaceful silence, passing a general store and then a saloon, each bearing posters for something called the Sheriff's Cup, which appeared to be some sort of local sporting contest. She made a mental note to stay clear of town on that day. There didn't seem to be a bookstore, Phoebe noticed sadly.

A woman in a scarlet gown, with long, pale tentacles streaming from her head sauntered out of the saloon as they passed, her eyes fixed on Tyro.

Phoebe felt a pang of sudden anger, shocked by how much it felt like jealousy.

Ugh, he's a guard, not a suitor. Chill out, Phoebe.

"Aren't you a big strong one?" the woman sang out to Tyro, wiggling her hips.

"Yes, thank you for noticing," he replied politely, looking at her eyes, not her bottom.

"I might even give you a discount," she tried again gamely.

"Great," he said. "What are you selling?"

The woman's eyes widened slightly and her tentacles fell flat to her shoulders.

Phoebe couldn't blame her disbelief. How dense could this guy be?

"Whatever you want," the woman replied in a sultry tone, eyeing him in a way that he surely couldn't misunderstand.

Phoebe saw the instant that Tyro recognized what was going on.

His eyebrows jumped up and he blushed an even deeper shade of green.

And somehow, in spite of everything, Phoebe began to laugh.

2

TYRO

Tyro turned in surprise.

The little Terran's sudden laughter was like a waterfall, sparkling and merry.

She had seemed so cold and unhappy until now.

It made the big warrior feel light inside to see that serious face alight with mirth, and he couldn't restrain his own laughter.

The situation was funny. He was a soldier, after all. And while he wasn't a regular of the brothels and pleasure ships, he should have recognized an invitation to pay for coupling.

The trouble was, he was so distracted by the curvy little Terran that he hadn't really paid much attention to anything going on around him.

First, he had horribly overpaid for groceries, and now he had dealt with a businesswoman as if he were an innocent dragonet instead of a grown man.

There was something about this Terran - something that was making his dragon behave strangely, pacing and groaning in his chest.

"My apologies," he said to the saloon woman, bowing as

low as he could with the baby in one arm and the unbelievably heavy trunk in the other.

"Don't worry about it," the woman said, looking a little miffed.

"We weren't laughing at you," he assured her solemnly. "We were laughing at me."

"I knew that," she replied in a warmer tone, winking. The pale tentacles on her head lifted once more, wiggling happily. "Come back and ask for Saana if you ever change your mind."

Satisfied that he had made things right, he turned back to the Terran.

"We should continue," he told her.

"Lead the way," she said.

He hadn't noticed before that her voice had a melodious quality. He wondered exactly where she was from. So many of the Terran planets had different dialects and accents.

He assumed she was from one of the lower Terras. A wealthier woman from one of the uppers would be unlikely to walk away from everything they knew to raise a child on a frontier moon.

Her amusement at bawdy humor supported his theory. He made a note to himself that she liked jokes. For some reason he couldn't explain, he was unusually interested in pleasing her.

"Would you like to know more about your son?" he asked her, belatedly remembering his manners.

"Yes, please," she said, eyeing the babe with an expression that almost looked suspicious.

"You may already know that the warriors of the Invicta are sworn to protect our homeland," he began.

"Yes, I've heard that," she said.

He wasn't sure, but he thought she was being sarcastic. He decided to ignore it.

"We once committed a tragic mistake that we cannot unmake," he said. "The details are unimportant, but as a result of our actions, the gentle society of Imber was destroyed. Recently, the Intergalactic Council ruled that the Invicta could use the preserved DNA of the lost Imberians to create pod babies. The babies will inherit all the mineral riches of their planet when they come of age. Until that time, the Invicta are sworn to guard them."

"Most of that was in the brochure," she said, nodding. "It doesn't explain why the baby is green."

"The people of Imber have chameleon-like abilities," he explained. "Because I have been his guard, Atlas has imprinted on me, so he shares my green coloring."

"And you're green because?"

"My own genetics," he told her. "Dragons of different lines have different skin tones and slightly different abilities. My green coloration and iridescent scales indicate my lineage."

He expected her to ask a follow-up about his abilities, after all, most Terrans viewed those as the most interesting thing about the dragon warriors.

Instead she walked on with a determined expression.

"I'm sure you're tired," he said after a moment.

"It was a rough flight," she admitted. "It will be good to get some rest."

The lights of the village had disappeared behind them and the docks were in sight now. It wouldn't be much longer.

"We're nearly there," he told her as he spotted the tent where they would spend the night.

His dragon roared at this and showed him a graphic image that made his heart forget to beat.

Mate, the dragon insisted.

That couldn't be right.

This strange little Terran couldn't be his mate.

But he closed his eyes and saw the image again.

His big green body covering hers, his hands tangled in her sun-colored hair, his cock sunk deep inside her, both of them screaming with pleasure.

Suddenly, the tent ahead of them seemed impossibly small.

3

PHOEBE

Phoebe glanced over at the big warrior.

He had gone quiet. She figured he must be tired too.

But then he met her eyes with a startled expression.

Something passed between them, though what it was she couldn't say. A tingle went down her spine, her cheeks burned, and a wave of longing swept over her.

No, Phoebe, no way.

She wrenched her eyes from his and focused on the stone road.

The last time she had let her hormones have anything to say about her actions, she had agreed to marry Cash Donavan, and look where that had gotten her - humiliated and off-planet with nothing but a big green baby and a trunk full of memories.

They walked on in silence for a few more minutes.

"Here we are," he boomed out, pointing ahead of them.

She followed his gaze. He seemed to be indicating a collection of wooden docks on the lake.

"We have to make another stop?" she asked.

"No, this is it," he told her. "That farm is all yours."

She blinked at him.

He looked pleased.

"Are you trying to make a joke?" she asked. "It's not funny. I'm tired."

"I'm not making a joke," he said, looking confused. "That's your farm."

"It's a dock, on a lake," she retorted. "I was promised land."

"I don't know what you were promised," he said. "But that's a luxberry farm, and a very good one from what I've been told. Did you ask if the land you were granted was submerged?"

"*Submerged,*" she echoed, horrified.

"That's how luxberries are grown," he said, entirely too calmly. "They have to be underwater. Come on, let's take a look."

She followed him helplessly onto the creaking wood of the dock, freezing in place when the whole thing shifted under her feet.

"What's wrong?" he asked.

"It feels like it's going to collapse," she spat.

"It's partially floating," he explained. "But it's very sturdy."

"How do you know?"

"Look at the age of the trees on this moon," he said, looking out at the wooded ridge that overlooked the village. "Nothing here will be flimsy until they run out of easy old-wood cuttings."

She scowled and took another step.

The dock moved under her feet, but when she thought of it as floating, it felt more stable.

A white tent had been set up a few yards onto the dock.

Beyond that sat crates of tools and implements she assumed were for growing or harvesting the berries.

"Can we stop at the house first?" she asked. "I'd like to lock up my stuff before we start looking at equipment."

"Sure," he said, continuing.

"Uh, where are you going?"

"The yurt," he said.

"The *what*?"

"The yurt, that's your home," he said. "It's a nice big one, too."

She blinked at the white tent. It was smaller than her wraparound porch back at the camellia farm.

But Tyro was already heading over to it, a delighted expression on his handsome face.

She was really starting to hate him.

"Come on, you'll love it," he called back to her.

She stomped down the deck, loathing every wobbly step of the journey. When she reached the tent, he was holding the door open for her. It had an actual door, that was a small comfort.

She stepped inside, prepared for the worst.

An unexpectedly spacious room awaited her. The walls were thick canvas, but the floor was piled with furs, and lanterns hung from the ceiling.

There was a huge bed, a small cradle, a sofa, and a small open kitchen with a cookstove and sink. It looked like a luxurious hotel suite, except that it was perfectly round with accordion marks on the walls.

"Do you love it?" Tyro asked quietly.

The question was impertinent.

But she did kind of love it. Or at least she didn't totally hate it.

"It looks like a circus tent," she said, unwilling to give him the satisfaction.

"It *does*," he realized out loud. "Atlas is going to grow up in a circus tent."

The gigantic baby was mercifully asleep on his shoulder. Phoebe didn't want his head being filled with a bunch of nonsense like that. Her own daddy had prepared her for a serious life from the very beginning.

And what good did it do me? I live in a circus tent, too.

She stifled a panicky giggle at such a ludicrous notion.

"Are you okay?" Tyro asked.

"It's been a long day," she said, pulling herself together. "When does the rest of the staff arrive? I could use a good meal."

"We don't have a staff," he said.

"What do you mean *we*?" she asked.

"I mean the three of us," he said, looking at her like she had just been thawed out of a deep-sleep.

"But you're not staying," she said. "You're just here to drop us off."

She assumed he'd be on his way as soon as he saw that they were settled in. Or whatever passed for settled into a tent.

"I'm here to guard the baby," he said.

"Well congratulations, you got him to me and you got me to my tent—"

"—yurt," he corrected her.

"*Yurt*," she echoed, balking at the sheer impropriety of it all. "At any rate, you've done what you had to do. We made it here safely. Now you can get out of this excuse for a farm."

"That's not how it works," he said softly.

And she could tell by his careful tone that something terrible was about to come next.

"It is my sworn duty to guard Atlas," he said. "Until he comes of age."

"Eighteen years?" Phoebe spluttered.

That was impossible. No one at the agency has ever said anything about spending eighteen years with a hulking dragon warrior that wouldn't stop smiling until you just wanted to slap him. Even if the smile did make her feel like the ground under her was shifting long before she stepped onto the floating dock.

"Actually, it's twenty," he said. "On Imber, the age of majority is twenty."

"Twenty years," she murmured to herself.

"And then I'm free to go," he said brightly.

"So I guess I do have a staff," she said, trying to see the bright side. "I have you."

"No, Atlas has me," he said quickly. "I don't work for you."

She let herself sink to the floor in total despair, face in her hands. This was not how she pictured her new life. Not at all.

"I know you're tired and hungry," he said, his voice gentle. "This will be easier for all of us if you and I make friends. Maybe we can help each other."

She looked up at him.

"My name is Tyro," he told her again as he offered her his hand. "What's yours?"

4

TYRO

Tyro held his breath, watching the fascinating creature before him try to make up her mind.

He hoped she would agree to open her heart to his friendship.

The dragon clearly wanted more than that, but it would have to do for now.

Her chocolate-colored eyes were so serious.

"You may address me as Miss…"

She hesitated for a moment, her eyes locked on his.

"Phoebe," she finished. "Just Phoebe, I think."

She was named for the sun. It suited her.

"It's nice to meet you, Phoebe," he said, smiling down at his golden-haired mate. "Would you like me to prepare you some dinner?"

She nodded, looking relieved, then took his hand and let him help her back to her feet.

"It would be my pleasure," he said, trying his best to ignore the jolt of sensation that shot through him as their hands touched. "Why don't you get comfortable? I'll try putting the baby down."

She nodded and looked around.

"Bathroom is usually behind the kitchen, because of the plumbing system," he said.

She headed to the door at the back of the kitchen and disappeared inside as he eased Atlas into the cradle. The baby was already sleeping hard after his afternoon outside. Fresh air really seemed to tucker the little guy out.

Tyro stroked the baby's soft cheek with a calloused finger, and then grabbed the sack of groceries and headed outside.

While there was a kitchen inside, he wanted to grill the produce. And he figured Phoebe could use a little time alone to adjust. Hopefully, when he returned with an incredible meal, she would be happier to see him.

Tyro made it to the end of the dock and stepped off onto the rocky beach. The fire pit there was a good size, and someone had left fuel for it. Before long, he had a nice fire crackling.

The sun was sinking fast, casting a pink glow on the surface of the lake. Phoebe must have figured out how to turn on the lamps. The yurt glowed like a beacon against the darkening sky.

He began unpacking the grocery sack. He extended a claw to slice fruit and vegetables, and then laid them on the grill to cook.

When he looked up from his task his breath caught in his throat.

Phoebe was clearly standing in front of one of the lanterns while changing out of that impractical purple gown.

Her graceful silhouette was visible in exquisite detail.

He knew he should run to the yurt and warn her that she was displaying herself to the world. The very thought that someone else might see her charms had a rumbling growl starting in his chest.

But they were on the far side of the lake, and there were no houses nearby.

He turned back slowly, in time to see his shadow mate lift her gown over her head, revealing round breasts with stiff nipples.

His body roared with need, the dragon inside commanding him to claim her.

Not yet, he told it inwardly.

Claim her before someone else does, it insisted.

That thought was unbearable. But still, he held back.

She was confused and unhappy. Claiming her would only add to the new situation that had overwhelmed her.

Claiming her would make her love her new situation.

He closed his eyes and saw his hands in her hair, heard her screams of ecstasy.

Not yet, he told himself firmly, opening his eyes. *First, I have to feed her.*

Tyro looked away and finished preparing their meal, singing to himself to stay focused. The song was one of the first Invicta marching cadences he had learned as a new soldier. It had bawdy lyrics and an upbeat melody.

One day maybe he would teach his mate the words. He hoped they would make her laugh, like she had laughed at his misunderstanding today.

It was a happy idea, and he was feeling at peace by the time he approached the yurt with a platter of steaming delicacies.

5

PHOEBE

Phoebe braced herself as the door opened.

She had spent more time than she was proud of wondering what he would think of her when she was wearing an everyday shift instead of that whorish purple gown the adoption agency had insisted she wear.

It was his fault. He was out there humming to himself in that deep, rumbly voice that somehow turned her insides to a blossoming meadow and her brains to mush.

I'm just tired and overwhelmed, she told herself. *Tomorrow I'll be myself again, and I won't have this misguided crush.*

But when he appeared in the doorway with a gigantic tray of fragrant food, it was hard not to find herself melting all over again.

"Are you ready to eat?" he asked.

His dark eyes danced with pleasure and she nearly lost herself in them.

"Very ready," she said, turning away from him so as not to encourage herself.

"Please, sit," he told her as he set the tray on the little

table and went back to close the door. "I'll find us something to drink."

She did as she was told. On the one hand, she wasn't usually one to follow orders. But on the other, he was serving her, which was something he had assured her he wasn't there to do. She didn't want to do anything that would make him remember.

He pulled out drawers and opened cupboards until he found what he wanted - plates, silverware, glasses, and an ancient looking bottle.

His armor didn't cover much of him. Those big muscles contracted and stretched as he moved with the grace of one of the big cats in the hologram films.

She felt her body warming at the sight and she bit her lip, hard.

"You okay, princess?" he asked.

His back was still to her, how did he know she was frustrated?

"Why do you keep calling me that?" she asked instead of answering.

"No reason," he said.

She huffed in indignation.

"Fine," he said, turning to her with that big, disarming smile. "You didn't tell me your name at first, and you seemed so... refined."

"Thank you," she said, pretending not to notice that he had surely been about to say a word that was less complimentary.

"You're welcome, princess," he said with a teasing half-smile.

"You know my name now," she reminded him.

"I do," he agreed. "You'll have wine with dinner, right?"

"Yes, please," she said.

He popped the cork on the bottle and poured slowly into the glasses.

The stipend she would be paid to tend to the little green orphan was minimal. She braced herself for the idea that this would be the last wine she would taste until she somehow got this ridiculous underwater berry farm turning a profit.

She wondered how long it would take her to earn the money to buy real land. The lush forest made it seem like an ideal spot for flower farming.

"Here you go, princess," Tyro said, leaning over her to place the glass in front of her.

He smelled like a wood fire.

Her mind transported her instantly back to her father's study, where a droid quietly added wood to the stove while her father read out loud to her from the almanac in his deep, gentle voice.

The scent reminded her of home so suddenly and so fully that she felt a pang in her chest and just managed to bite back a sob.

"What's wrong?" he asked, going down on one knee in front of her, and placing one of his massive hands on her shoulder.

A frisson of longing went through her, and she could see his eyes going hazy with lust.

"What's happening to me?" she murmured. Hot tears gathered in her eyes.

Tyro pulled his hand away, as if he had touched a hot iron.

"Let's eat," he said lightly. "Then we can get to know each other better."

He straightened and began piling food onto a plate for

her before she had a chance to tell him that she didn't want to know him better.

But the truth was she *did* want to know him better, *much* better than would be proper to say out loud. And that made her angry. And sad. And lonely, too.

When he placed her meal in front of her, she managed to distract herself from her emotions with the beauty of the colorful feast.

"I put the vegetables in order of flavor," he told her. "So start on the left for the more mild stuff, and then you can work your way to the right if you like spicy and bitter foods."

He wasn't the boss of her.

She stabbed a slice of something green at the far-right side of the plate.

"Oh no, not that," he said.

But she had already shoved it into her mouth.

The texture was crispy and refreshing.

But as she chewed, the flavor went swiftly from watery to fiery. One moment she was appreciating the spice, the next, her head was on fire.

Her expression must have shown her agony. Tyro began to laugh, a deep, rumbly laugh that embraced her, even as she desperately grabbed for her wine.

"Oh, no, that won't help," he told her, hopping up and reaching for something she couldn't see.

Her mouth was turning inside out. Even her nose was burning.

Tyro returned with a cell of the milk meant for baby Atlas.

She didn't even protest that she wasn't a baby, or ask what kind of animal the milk had come from.

She just took it from him with shaking hands and

proceeded to splash half of it all over herself while trying to get it to her mouth.

"Let me help you, princess," he laughed and held it to her lips.

The first drops of sweet milk began to instantly put out the fire in her mouth.

But that left her to take in the sight of the big green warrior towering above her, holding something to her mouth as he fixed her with those dark eyes.

What has gotten into you, Phoebe?

She almost laughed, which caused her to choke a little.

Instantly, he pulled the cell away from her and knelt in front of her again.

"Are you okay?" he asked.

"I'm fine," she said. "Really, I'm fine."

"Why did you eat that whole monster apple?" he asked.

"Because you told me not to," she replied honestly.

"I thought we were friends," he said, chuckling. "Why not take my advice?"

"No one tells me what to do," she said, shrugging.

"Even when I'm trying to help you have a good time?" he asked.

Her whole body clenched with need at the thought of a good time with him. But he didn't appear to have chosen suggestive words on purpose.

Damn her stupid hormones.

"Let's just eat," she said.

He nodded and went back to his place.

She grabbed her fork and went straight for the pale stuff on the far-left side of her plate.

"Good girl," he said. "That's butter pear. It's everyone's favorite."

It was well named. The sweet, buttery fruit burst with

flavor in her mouth. She closed her eyes to enjoy it, moaning in relief.

When she opened them, he was staring at her, his jaw clenched.

"That's really good," she said, wondering why he looked half-angry. "Can you grow it underwater?"

"Sadly, no," he told her. "And the soil near the lake is too rocky. These are grown up on the ridge."

She nodded and tried the next item on the left. It was red and a little mushy.

The flavor reminded her of the spiced beverage one of the droids from the inner ring used to prepare for her father.

"Do you like it?" Tyro asked.

"It reminds me of inner ring tea," she told him.

"Interesting," he said. "Most Terrans say it reminds them of sweet potatoes. That's called caroote. It's a root vegetable, but we always sprinkle it with cinnamon."

They continued their meal, with Tyro explaining the names and origins of the various foods.

Most of them were delicious. Phoebe had always been an adventurous eater, and even the most bitter and spicy choices were fun to try.

When they were finished with the produce, he brought out two thick slices of something that looked a lot like cake.

"What is this?" she asked, waiting for another exotic explanation.

"Cake," he told her, confirming her more mundane suspicions. "Made from nut flour, burden moose butter, and honey, with a butter pear glaze."

The first bite was pure heaven.

"Is this how everyone on this moon eats?" she asked, trying to pace herself and savor the treat.

"Not every day," he laughed. "This meal was to introduce you to all the flavors of Clotho. But it was expensive."

"How expensive?" she asked, hoping he hadn't spent her whole food budget in one night.

"It was my treat," he told her. "So don't worry about it. And we can get a lot of these things at the weekly farmer's market for less if you like them. It's more expensive in the shops."

She nodded. The same was true of the open flower market on Terra 212.

"Let me get these," he said, picking up his plate and reaching for hers.

"No," she said, resigned. "You're here for Atlas, not for me. I'll clean up my own dish."

He blinked in surprise and she was pretty sure he was going to say something to tease her. She hopped up with her plate and the tray before he had the chance.

When she reached the kitchen sink, she looked around in confusion.

The droids took care of all her needs back home, except when she was on an all-night reading streak, and got up in the wee hours for a glass of wine.

The kitchen at home had a ready-hot for tea, a compactor for garbage and a compost funnel so that unwanted food stuffs could be used as fertilizer for the flowers. They had a pretty turquoise washer unit with shelves to place soiled dishes on for cleaning.

This kitchen was just a sink, a stovetop, and a bunch of cupboards.

The only thing that was even remotely familiar was the small camellia plant that she'd place in a pot near the window. It looked about as wilted as she felt.

She looked around, wondering what she was supposed to do.

"How about you watch me this time and help me next time?" Tyro's deep voice said from right behind her.

She turned to him.

He was standing close, so close that she could feel the heat pouring off him.

The Invicta were dragon warriors - everyone knew that. But she had never thought about what that meant.

The man in front of her wasn't really a man, beneath the scant armor and bristling muscles lurked a fire-breathing beast.

And she found the idea excited her.

"Here," he murmured, as if he too were under the strange spell.

He took the plates from her, and put his arms around her to turn on the taps of the sink.

She spun around in the cage of his arms to see what he was doing with the dishes.

He ran his hand in front of the sensor to release a cascade of bubbles, then slowly dragged a sponge over the surface of her plate, covering it in delicate foam before plunging it into the warm water.

She kept expecting him to shatter the delicate dishes. But his big hands were surprisingly gentle.

"Now you do mine," he murmured.

His hot whisper left her weak-kneed enough that suddenly she didn't mind doing a droid's job. She was determined to do it well enough to please him.

She released the soap bubbles onto the plate and drifted the sponge over it. But she could still see residue on the surface.

"Harder," he whispered. "Like this."

The next thing she knew, his big hands were wrapping around hers.

He was so warm, and he still smelled of the wood fire and the wind.

His whole body was wrapped around hers now, she could feel his warmth everywhere, the hard planes of his chest against her shoulder blades, the stiff length of him pressed to her posterior, evidence that she wasn't alone in this ocean of desire.

She forgot where she was, allowing his hands to guide hers through the warm, soapy water as she lost herself in his embrace.

"There," he said at last, the clink of the plate on the counter signaling that it was over.

She spun around in his arms and gazed up into his beautiful, dark eyes.

"Phoebe." He said her name like a prayer.

She placed her open palms on his chest, relishing the light sizzle of electricity that moved between them at this touch.

"Gods, woman," he groaned.

But instead of wrapping his arms around her and bending to kiss her, he effortlessly trapped her wrists in one big hand, pulling them from his chest.

She heard the whimpering sound in her throat before she realized she was going to make it. Her cheeks were hot with shame.

She had misread the situation and thrown herself at a man who was here to guard a baby, not to seduce its thoughtless new mother.

"I'm sorry," she whispered, looking away from him.

"No," he murmured, cupping her cheek in his hand, guiding her to look up at him once more. "Everything you are feeling is right. I feel it too. I only want to be sure you understand it."

"What is there to understand?" she asked. "I'm a woman, you're a man, and we are both young and healthy. My father explained all of it to me when I was a child."

He blinked at her in surprise.

"What?" she asked.

"So you think that every man and woman feel what we're feeling right now?" he asked.

She shrugged.

"Is this what it's been like for you with other men?" he asked.

"There haven't been any other men," she said lightly, hoping he wasn't going to make a *thing* out of it.

He sucked in a breath, and when she looked up at him again, she could see the tension in his jaw.

"Good," he said. "I'm glad. How much do you know about dragon shifters?"

"You're dangerous, but disciplined," she said, "and bigger than average men, even in humanoid form. You're protective, and have hot tempers."

"Do you know about the mate bond?" he asked.

Oh.

"Not really," she admitted.

She knew there were plenty of races and cultures in the stars who had fated mates, mate bonds, and even the opposite - mates who destroyed each other or died after joining.

Intending to stay single, she had never paid much attention to these stories. She wondered what he needed to tell her that was so important.

But the pull of his body was so great that she wondered if she would be able to resist, even if he told her he would have to cook her and eat her afterward.

He was holding her hands gently now, no longer cuffing her wrists. That would make it easier to escape, if she could convince herself to try.

"Dragons mate for life," he told her simply.

She wasn't expecting that.

He gazed down at her, as if waiting for a response.

"Oh," she said stupidly.

"What that means, princess," he told her, "is that if we act on our desire, you'll be mine forever."

"F-forever?"

"It will be my honor to guard you from harm, care for you and our young, and pleasure you in every possible way, for the rest of your life," he explained, reaching out to stroke her cheek.

His big hand was featherlight against her sensitive skin.

Phoebe felt light-headed with desire.

This isn't what I want.

I want my independence.

I want to answer to no one.

But all her life mottos just sounded like a bunch of words in random order to her now.

The only thing she wanted was to lay claim to this man.

"I will not claim you tonight," he told her, letting go of her hands. "Get some rest and we can talk about it in the morning."

She was left bereft and speechless as he broke contact, grabbed his pack, and headed out the door of the yurt, leaving her alone with her thoughts.

As if on cue, the baby began to wail.

"Wait," she said softly, a moment too late for him to hear.

6

PHOEBE

Phoebe stood in the center of the yurt, holding the baby for the first time.

He was surprisingly heavy. She hadn't anticipated that part.

At first, he had felt about right for a baby, but the longer she held him, the heavier he seemed to get. She wondered if it was something about him being Imberian, like maybe they had the ability to change their mass. If so, Tyro hadn't warned her.

At least the baby had stopped crying when she picked him up, which was encouraging. Now he was eyeing her suspiciously, hiccuping and sniffling instead of wailing.

"What do you want?" she asked him, in a friendly way.

But he didn't answer. Which checked out. He was a baby after all.

"There are cells of milk in the ice box," she remembered out loud.

She shifted the boulder of a baby into the crook of her left arm. He got a stormy look on his face, but he didn't cry.

"Good," she told him. "You're okay. We're going to find you some dinner. I was grumpy before mine, too."

She headed to the kitchen to get his milk.

The cell in the icebox was very cold.

She was pretty sure she wasn't supposed to serve it to him that way.

But now that Tyro was gone and her hormones were cooling off, she didn't want to drag him back in here to help her.

No. It would be better to figure this out on her own.

"How would I warm up milk?" she wondered out loud.

The stove top couldn't be that hard to use.

She grabbed a pan and filled it with water, then placed the milk cell in the water. This was how she had seen the droids heat up the clay for her art projects back at home.

The stove top turned on with her first try.

The only thing was to get the milk warm but not hot enough to burn the baby's mouth.

He began to cry again, as if at the idea.

"Don't worry, we'll figure it out," she told him firmly as he banged his head on her shoulder. "There's no need to head butt me. I'm trying to do you a favor here."

The water on the stove top began bubbling slightly.

"Crap," she said, turning off the heat.

She paced the floors with the crying baby, waiting for the water to cool a little.

At last she could plunge her hand into the water to retrieve the cell.

It was warm to the touch, so she put it back in the ice box, hoping to cool it down faster that way.

Suddenly, the baby went quiet.

She could feel his little body tightening as if he were preparing to make a run for it.

Then he relaxed.

Thank God...

She caught a whiff of something awful in the air.

Terrified that it was spoiled milk, she opened the ice box.

But the milk smelled sweet and fine, though it was still a little too warm to feed to the baby.

The bad smell in the air, however, was only growing stronger.

"Rings of Saturn, did you poop?" she asked Atlas.

He laughed at her.

Good Lord, what was she supposed to do now?

There were no droids, no servants, no one but Tyro. And she couldn't go out there and face him again. She just couldn't.

Phoebe struggled to remember anything from the brief instructions the agency had given them. But she had never really considered that she might be the one performing those duties, so she honestly hadn't been paying much attention. Their insistence on making all the prospective mothers sit through those dreadful presentations made much more sense to her now.

There was a bag component to the baby's cradle. Maybe there would be something in there to help.

Wrinkling her nose against the worsening smell, she knelt to open the bag.

After the better part of an hour, and more effort than she would have thought possible, Phoebe was exhausted but triumphant.

Sure, removing the baby's soiled undergarment had left both of them disgusting.

And yes, she had left the milk in the ice box too long and had to rewarm it.

And while she was doing that, the baby had peed on her, since she had not put more garments on him.

But now they were relaxing in a warm bathtub, both of them clean again, and the baby contentedly downing his milk, which she had brought to the right temperature by putting it in the bath tub with them.

She was very sure she hadn't done things exactly the right way, but they were figuring it out.

And he seemed pretty happy now. Which made her feel much happier than she expected it to.

He smacked her cheek with a chubby fist as if to tell her she was on the right track.

"You really are going to be a full-time job," she told him.

He let the cell out of his mouth long enough to burp loudly and then latch on again.

By the time the milk was gone, she could tell he was very sleepy. She didn't blame him. Their ordeal had been exhausting.

She got them both out of the tub, then dried him off and diapered him as quickly as possible, so as not to have to start all over again.

Then she dried herself off and put on a sleeping gown.

The baby whimpered the first few times she tried to put him down.

But when she hummed a song to him, he calmed a bit and his tiny eyelids began to droop. He was awfully cute, even though he was excessively green.

At last, he allowed her to place him in his cradle without a fuss.

Phoebe sighed in relief, looking around to try to decide what to do first. The trouble was, she was just as tired as he was.

After a few minutes of trying to convince herself she

could stay up, she gave up on getting anything else done, turned off all the lanterns, and crawled into her own bed.

Tomorrow, she would take inventory of the house, as well as the farm and its equipment.

Maybe they could even go back into town and rent a droid, ideally a nice big one. They had passed a machine workshop that surely would have droids to rent.

Labor was an important component to a well-run farm, second only to flawless planning.

She wondered if she could find a good text to help her learn more about these berries and what she needed to do to tend to them.

Though she expected to be up all night worrying and planning, she felt herself drifting off almost immediately after pulling up the covers.

In her dream, Phoebe was warm, so warm.

Sunlight bathed her naked limbs and the scent of coconut butter soothed her sense.

The ocean lapped against the sands of the Ordish coastline and the breeze gently rustled the fronds of the palm trees.

She opened her eyes to see the water, such an intense teal-blue that it almost hurt to look at it. A frothy wave crashed against the shore and from it rose a god.

No, not a god.

It was Tyro, emerging from the blue-green depths, droplets clinging to his long, dark hair, and sliding down his naked, muscular form, exactly the way she wanted to run her hands down it.

His dark eyes fixed on hers.

Phoebe was normally shy about her voluptuous figure. But instead of wanting to cover herself, she found herself wishing she could bare herself further, show him the inside of her heart, peel off the layers of her very soul.

He drew closer until he blocked the sun and she was completely embraced by his shade.

He regarded her for just a moment, then lowered himself to the sand at her feet.

Otherworldly music filled her ears.

His dark eyes flashed emerald, and he pressed his lips to her thighs without breaking eye contact.

She felt herself lifting, ready to combust or levitate - something, anything to ease the ache his warm mouth had awoken.

He pressed kisses to her belly, her clavicle, her cheeks.

Her body wept and sang for him.

You are my mate, he told her again without speaking. *But I will not claim you. Not until you beg.*

She opened her mouth, ready to plead.

But no sound would come.

A lazy smile appeared on his handsome face.

I'll ask again another day.

She closed her eyes as he trailed kisses down to her breasts, until she was sure she wouldn't survive this torture.

"Phoebe," he said aloud, nuzzling around her pebbled nipple without touching it.

She sank her fingers into the sand in frustration.

But the sand behaved oddly, swirling around her hands instead of breaking away under them.

"Phoebe," he said, again, sounding worried.

There was an odd knocking sound.

She opened her eyes to find she was in her bed beside the cradle.

Pink sunrise bled in through the walls of the yurt.

The front door opened before she could pull it together enough to answer.

"Are you okay?" Tyro asked, bursting in.

"Yes, I was just sleeping," she murmured, trying to cover herself in the sheets before remembering that she wasn't actually naked. Her sleeping gown covered more of her than that purple number she had been wearing when she met him. "What do you want?"

"Sorry," he said, his voice rough. "I had a dream that you needed me."

You don't know the half of it, buddy.

"I won't be sleeping out there anymore," he said decidedly. "I'll sleep on the floor in here."

She stifled a groan.

If she was having sex dreams about him when he was outside, how was she supposed to sleep with him right next to her?

"Go back to sleep," he told her. "I'll get up with Atlas when he wakes."

Before she could get her brain moving fast enough to argue, he was stretched out on the fur rug beside the cradle.

She had no choice but to close her eyes and beg her body to stop pounding with need long enough for her to get some sleep.

7
PHOEBE

Phoebe awoke feeling cranky.

She opened her eyes and looked around, but Tyro and Atlas were nowhere to be found.

Her body was still humming with need and she wondered briefly if she dared take care of that herself while they were gone.

But all she could think of was Tyro bursting in again and catching her in the act.

I'm in control of my hormones, they're not in control of me, she told herself proudly.

She washed up quickly and dressed.

The boys still weren't back when she emerged from the bathroom, so she headed out the front door, hoping they hadn't gone to town without her.

The sun was brilliant overhead, and its reflection on the water made the lake look as if it were filled with diamonds.

She spotted Tyro right away, standing out on the far end of the dock with Atlas in his arms.

With the sun coming up behind him and the water

sparkling all around, he reminded her of the godlike version of him that had been in her dream.

She shivered once and then shook her head.

Get ahold of yourself, Phoebe. It was just a dream.

She strode purposefully down the dock, willing herself to fix her mind on business.

"Good morning," Tyro called to her.

She gave him a little wave.

As she got closer, she realized he had spread out the parts of some sort of machine across the dock. The metal shimmered in the sunlight like fish scales.

"What's this?" she asked.

"Something's missing," he told her. "I tried to start the pump, but it didn't work."

"What's missing?" she asked.

"The pump impeller," he replied, crouching over the parts again. "Did you notice if it was here last night?"

"Oh, sure, I remember checking on that specifically," she said. "First, I wanted to figure out where I was going to sleep, since there didn't seem to be a house on my farm, or a farm, for that matter. But as soon as I got that sorted, my exact next thought was to make sure the pump impeller was right where it belonged. I checked it first thing."

"Was it here?" he asked.

She gaped at him, unbelieving.

He leaned in slightly, as if anticipating her answer.

"Are you insane?" she yelled. "Of course I don't know if it was here or not. Why would I know that? I don't even know what it is."

He laughed heartily.

"That was a very good joke, Phoebe," he said, after a moment, panting. "My people do not often recognize sarcasm, so at first I was fooled. But now I understand the humor."

"You don't *recognize sarcasm*?" she echoed.

"The Invicta are very much opposed to sarcasm in all its forms," he explained solemnly. "They say that its use indicates dishonor. But they have not experienced the humor of it as I have, just now."

"Is it a problem that this part is missing?" she asked, eager to change the subject. Her daddy didn't like sarcasm either, and this conversation made her miss him.

"Without the impeller, the pump won't work," Tyro said. "And without a working pump, we can't harvest the berries. So it's a terrible problem, but one with a solution. We'll just have to buy another pump impeller."

"Will they have it in town?" she asked.

"They should," he told her. "Sometimes on these frontier moons, you have to order parts and wait for them. But there are enough other farmers on this lake that I would guess they keep them in stock."

"Good," she said, nodding. "Let's go now. I was hoping we could rent a droid too."

"A droid?" he asked.

"Yes, to help with the farming," she said. "Labor is one of the most important components on a farm."

"We can probably look at droids, sure," he said.

Atlas squeaked and waved his fingers at her.

"Someone wants his mama," Tyro said delightedly. "Did you two have a nice night?"

"We did," she said, surprised to find herself extremely eager to take the green baby into her arms again.

He was heavy, but it was a good heavy.

He grabbed a fistful of her hair and leaned his little green head forward to bump hers.

"Hi, Atlas," she murmured, feeling like her heart might actually melt.

"Bah," he squeaked.

"Ready to go for a walk to town?" she asked him.

He didn't answer, mostly because he was a baby, but partly because he was too busy trying to fit his fist in his mouth. Luckily, it was the fist that didn't have a hank of her hair in it.

Together, they set off down the dock toward the path back to the village. They had walked for a minute or two when something hit her.

"Do you think the part was just missing from our pump, or do you think someone took it?" she asked Tyro.

"It was a used pump," he said. "So I'm guessing it was taken."

Her mind went to her trunk, still sitting in the yurt and her heart pounded with fear.

It would be so easy to break into that yurt - anyone with a knife and a few minutes to spare could walk right in and help themselves to whatever they wanted.

"I'm going to need some other things when we get to town," she said, her mind working a mile a minute.

Was it safe to leave the trunk long enough for a quick walk to town?

She glanced around, but saw no sign of anyone else.

Instinct told her not to make a big deal out of it. If she asked Tyro to carry it along with them, he would know there was more in there than she was letting on.

As long as they were quick, everything would be fine.

"Everything okay?" he asked her.

She nodded, buttoning her lips and vowing to make this the quickest trip to town ever.

8

TYRO

Tyro tried to concentrate on his task.

The sunlight was warm, the day was new, and all was well. He only had to keep the baby safe.

And now the mother, too, since he was sure she was his mate.

Keeping an eye out for danger was all he had to accomplish.

But it was so hard to stay alert with the scent of her arousal still mesmerizing his senses.

He had awoken at dawn from a dream in which she screamed his name, begging and pleading for something. Terrified, he had leapt to his feet and pounded down the dock to the yurt. He'd burst in the door to find her tossing in her sheets, frantic with lust.

And while he stood there frozen, begging his dragon not to take her while she slept, she had awoken and asked what he wanted.

What do you want?

Like she was taking his order in a damned diner.

You, I want you, he had wanted to scream back.

But if she was determined to ignore her own need, he would have to ignore his, though the flames licked at him cruelly.

So he had stretched out on her floor and stared at the ceiling until the babe awoke.

"Will they have chain here?" she asked, indicating the general store.

"Sure," he said. "How much do you need?"

"I want two meters of it, plus something we can use to anchor it to the dock," she explained. "I want to secure my trunk, in case there are thieves around."

"Most likely they only took something they needed," Tyro said quietly. "Probably while they thought the farm was abandoned."

"Nonetheless," she said. "I want to secure my belongings."

"Of course," he told her as they stepped inside.

He waited for his eyes to adjust to the dim interior, using his other senses to keep tabs on Phoebe and Atlas while he did.

The store had its usual smells of oil, metal, wood chips, dried meat, and the almost-sweet body odor of its owner, a Fibbian by the name of Cronx. Tyro had befriended the gregarious shop keeper on his initial trip to scout the farm location for security purposes.

He expected Phoebe to have her eyes fixed on the spools of metal chain behind the counter. Instead, she was carefully examining a set of plastic wrenches.

That was odd. They had a real titanium wrench set back at the dock, and she had seen it, because Tyro had used it to disassemble the pump, it had been sitting out beside the parts. But a lot of the farmers probably used the plastic sets. They were cheaper, and when you inevitably dropped one in the lake, they floated. His titanium wrenches did not, a fact he'd discovered for himself this morning.

Maybe Phoebe already knew this. She was the one that was supposed to be knowledgeable in the ways of farming.

"Tyro," Cronx cried, waving all four of his arms.

"Hello, Cronx," Tyro said politely. "How is your family?"

Cronx waved his arms to indicate two small Fibbians playing jax cubes in the corner of the store, their mother watching over them with a novel in her hands.

"Wonderful, sir," Cronx said. "And I see your family is growing."

"This is Phoebe, and that's Atlas she's holding," Tyro said, not wanting to highlight his relationship, or lack of a relationship, with Phoebe. "We need some sturdy chain."

Phoebe shot him an angry look. He probably should have specified that she wasn't in his family.

But he knew she would be soon, if their bodies had any say in the matter.

"Of course," Cronx boomed, moving to the spools. "What is it for?"

Tyro opened his mouth to answer, but Phoebe beat him to it.

"Chaining farming equipment," she said. "It needs to be strong enough that it can't be cut through with common tools."

"Ah," Cronx said. "This should do. How many meters would you like?"

Phoebe narrowed her eyes at the spool Cronx was pointing to.

"Two, please," Tyro said, glad he remembered how much she wanted.

"And we'll need an implement to cut it with," Phoebe said quickly. "Bolt cutters, maybe?"

"Sure, we have those," Cronx said in a cheerful way.

"Then that's the wrong chain," Phoebe said in a loud, clear voice.

Cronx blinked at her.

"We need chain that can't be cut," Phoebe said sweetly. "Did I mention that?"

"Trouble is, that kind of chain is very expensive," Cronx said.

"We don't care," Tyro said quickly. "She wants what she wants."

Cronx smiled and turned back to the spools.

Phoebe turned to Tyro with a furious look.

He shrugged. The owner had only been trying to save them credits.

"Here you go," Cronx said, pointing to a spool in the corner with dust hanging from it. "This is thick alloy with flattened links that distribute pressure. It's not impossible to cut if you have industrial tools. But it's the best thing on this moon."

Tyro glanced at Phoebe, who was nodding.

"Only trouble is, it's probably more valuable than whatever you're trying to chain up," Cronx chuckled.

"Looks like you've got quite a bit of it," Phoebe said. "I guess it doesn't sell as well as you'd hoped."

"When people need it, they really need it," Cronx replied. He pointed at the price tag.

Tyro's eyes nearly popped out of his head.

He was glad he had ample savings.

"We don't really need it," Phoebe said, turning on her heel.

"We'll take two meters," Tyro said, glad he could provide for her, even if the chain was more than she could afford herself.

"Tyro," she said, sounding more irritated than grateful.

"It's my pleasure," he told her.

She nodded and waited while he paid.

They both watched as Cronx measured out the length of chain and then used industrial cutters to remove it. Even with the superior equipment, it took time. Not many people on all of Clotho would be able to manage that.

Phoebe stayed quiet as Tyro and Cronx chose an anchor and lock that could withstand the same level of punishment.

"Thank you for your patronage," Cronx called to them as they left.

Tyro waved to him and to his family.

When he turned back to Phoebe, he realized she had marched on ahead.

"Phoebe, what's wrong?" he asked, jogging to catch up.

"Don't they haggle on these frontier moons," she muttered to herself.

"Of course," he told her. "But we don't need to do that. I have savings."

"How long are they supposed to last if you keep overpaying for everything?" she asked. "That chain had been on his wall for years. You could have gotten a discount of at least twenty percent and he still would have been happy."

"But he has a wife and children to support," Tyro said. "Those poor kids were playing jax cubes on the floor. He needs the money."

"Children love playing jax cubes on the floor," Phoebe retorted. "Besides, did you see his wife's earrings? They were pure electrum, and she had a matching bangle. He's doing fine."

"Oh," Tyro said.

It was true. He hadn't noticed the jewelry.

And he supposed she was right about the children. He had fond memories of playing jax cubes under the table himself as a small boy.

"I'll tell you what," Phoebe said, her eyes sparkling. "Let me do the talking at the equipment place."

"But you don't really know what we're looking for," he said.

"A pump impeller," she said without hesitation. "For luxberry farming."

"Okay," he said, nodding. "Just squeeze my arm if you need me to bail you out, and I'll take over."

"It's a deal," she told him.

They had reached the huge metal building that housed the heavy equipment that was sold and leased on Clotho. Droids sailed in and out, carrying heavy items and assisting customers.

"May I help you, madam?" one of the smaller droids asked, sailing up to them.

"No, thank you," she replied.

Tyro was surprised, but didn't say anything. He had agreed to keep quiet.

When the droid was gone, she turned to him.

"Take me to where the part should be," she told him. "But take the scenic route. We need to look at other things first."

He nodded and they walked into the entry area.

There were seedlings in pots and he followed her lead when she examined them carefully.

Next, they headed deeper into the store and viewed several rows of tarps and coverings.

Small tools and nuts and bolts were next.

As she examined them, he understood what she had been doing with the wrenches in the last shop. She was convincing the owner that her interest was in one area, when it was really in another all along.

Very clever.

At last, he brought her to the section where parts for the pump could be found, behind a locked glass case.

"Which one do we need?" she asked. "Do they have it?"

He nodded at the item in question. It was unimpressive looking. If he hadn't known what it was, it would have looked like a simple plastic tube with something sticking out of each end.

In reality, their entire operation would be useless without it.

"There are two," he said.

"Thank God," she replied under her breath.

Another droid sailed up to them.

She immediately fixed her eyes on a different part.

"May I help you, madam?" it asked.

"No, thank you, just looking," she replied.

It sailed away again, leaving Tyro completely confused.

"Hello there, friends," a man said, stepping up behind the counter. "I'll bet you like good old fashioned customer service better than those pesky droids."

Phoebe turned to the man with a radiant smile. "Oh, thank you," she said. "We're mostly here to compare prices, but those droids can be so pushy."

"Indeed," the salesman said with a pleased smile. "But I don't know that you can compare prices. We're the only equipment shop on Clotho at the moment."

"Yes, but I have a sister off-moon," Phoebe said. "She's planning a visit and she can bring whatever I need. Isn't that lucky? But of course I'd rather buy local."

"We appreciate that," he replied, with a slight bow, looking less pleased.

"Now what can you tell me about this?" she asked, pointing at the sensor she had pretended to view when the droid approached them.

"Ah, that's the sensor," the salesman said. "It's waterproof, a necessity when it comes to luxberries."

"How much?" Phoebe asked.

"Four hundred eighty credits," he replied.

"That seems like a lot," Phoebe replied, eyes wide.

"It's exclusive to luxberry harvesting," the salesman explained. "That means they don't produce as many, and therefore it's more expensive. We really don't have much of a mark-up on it, like we do other things."

"So you can't give me a special price?" she asked.

"I'm sorry, my dear," he told her. "If only you needed another part, I could give you a twenty-five percent discount. But the sensor is very specialized."

Tyro's mouth fell open.

Phoebe tapped his foot with hers and he shut it again.

"You could give me a twenty-five percent discount on another part?" she echoed.

"Sure," he said, quickly.

"On *any* of the parts in this case," she said.

"Except that one," he repeated. "I'm very sorry, madam. Would you like me to box it up for you?"

"May I see that?" she asked, pointing to the impeller.

"That's a pump impeller," he told her. "But the pump won't work without a sensor."

"I'll take them both," she said.

"The sensor and the impeller?" he asked.

"Both impellers," she said. "Please box them up carefully."

His face went slack.

"Thank you so much," she added warmly. "The discount

will be such a help, and I'm sure my sister can secure a sensor for me before her visit. If not, I'll be back and see you again."

His face twisted into a smile that made it look a bit like he had a toothache. But he boxed up the two parts carefully, took her credits, and handed the package over.

"Will there be anything else?" he asked.

"The shiny droid by the entry, what does it rent for?" she asked.

"Oh, that's an expensive machine," he said.

"How much?"

"Eighty credits per week," he told her.

"And the little one?"

"Fifteen credits per week, but it can't plant or harvest," he said with a smile.

"I'll take the little one," she said.

"It needs service," he told her.

"I can service it," she said. "If you can reduce the rent to twelve per week."

"Absolutely not," he said.

"Understood," she told him. "You have a nice day."

"Wait," he said. "Fourteen per week for the first month if you service it. Fifteen after that."

"Fantastic," she said, her face lighting up.

He bent to retrieve an ownership disc from behind the counter.

"You'll pay the first month up front," he said, handing it to her.

"Thank you again," she said, handing him more credits with another big smile. "You have been so kind."

He smiled a little more genuinely this time. "Bring luck on Clotho," he told her.

Tyro turned to her, amazed.

She winked at him, and then they headed away from the counter.

The people who had been in line behind them were whispering, and not all of it was kind, but Tyro didn't care.

His mate was very, very clever.

And it filled him with pride.

9

PHOEBE

Phoebe kept her arms wrapped protectively around Atlas as they exited the store.

While she was proud of the lessons in commerce she had learned at her father's side, she was suddenly aware that her skill was a double-edged sword.

The whispers around them were too low for her to make out completely, but their tone was clear.

The other citizens of Clotho didn't appreciate her coming in and buying up equipment.

They didn't appreciate her being here at all.

She focused on getting out of the store, out of range of the whispers and stares.

When they reached the droid, she inserted the ownership disk and it lit up. She set it to silent follow mode so as not to gain any more unwanted attention.

Though it needed service, it was a good-looking piece of machinery, sturdy and reasonably maintained. She was sure she could teach it to do just about anything she wanted.

But right now, she only wanted a fast getaway.

She turned and headed for the exit with both Tyro and the droid in tow.

"You were amazing," Tyro told her as soon as they reached the street. "Now I understand why you wanted to handle our business affairs. From here on in, you will. We should go to the saloon and have a hearty lunch to celebrate."

"We need to go home," she told him. "Right away."

He frowned, but stayed by her side as she headed back toward their dock. Once they were on the edge of the village, she turned to him.

"What were they saying?" she asked.

"What do you mean?" His voice was guarded and he didn't meet her eyes.

He was clearly just trying to spare her feelings.

"I know they were saying bad things about me," she clarified. "And I bet your dragon has good enough hearing that you know exactly what they said."

"Phoebe, do you know what they tell the young dragonets about listening in with enhanced senses?" he asked.

"If you listen at doors, you hear what you deserve?" she offered, remembering that phrase from her own childhood.

"Basically that, yes," he said. "If those people whispered, it means they weren't trying to confront you, Phoebe. And you have a lifetime to prove them wrong."

"Please just tell me," she said. "I want to be prepared. I need to know what I'm up against."

He sighed.

"Please," she repeated.

"You won't hold it against me?" he asked.

"You're just the messenger," she told him.

He looked around them, and she did the same. But they were completely alone.

"Here's the thing, Phoebe," he said. "All the complaints basically add up to this. The best docks on the lake were set aside for you. The best local berries were seeded in the lake for you."

"I didn't ask for that," she said. "I didn't want a dock at all."

"I know that," he told her. "But to the locals, it seems like you're starting off with an unfair advantage in the market. We even bought the last two impellers today, when we only needed one."

"I was afraid it would be stolen again," she admitted, suddenly feeling much less pleased with her own cleverness.

"They're afraid that with the advantages you appear to have, real or not, you'll do very well," he said. "And then more like you will come. One woman seemed sure the tax man would soon raise the property taxes to drive the locals out, and that none of the old wet-farmers would be able to hang on. Her friend agreed that within a year, only the upper crust from off-moon would inhabit the farms on the lake.'"

"That's awful," she said. "That's not what I want at all."

"I know that," he said. "And soon, they'll know that too."

"But in the interim, they'll try to sabotage me," she went on. "And they'll probably succeed, since I don't know what I'm doing."

Tyro's jaw clenched, but he didn't argue.

"A stop for lunch sounds great," she said. "But for now, I think it's more important to go back, lock down my stuff, and inventory the farm equipment before any more of it gets stolen."

"Agreed," he said after a moment. "Let's get home and lock everything down."

She felt a pang of relief that he wasn't going to try to spare her feelings or save his own efforts.

He's my mate. He has my back, a voice in the back of her head said with satisfaction.

A shiver of anticipation went down her spine as her thoughts turned back to the dream from last night. She glanced over at Tyro, who was trying to hide a half smile.

"What?" she asked.

"It's just that, my kind doesn't really try to hide their, uh, emotions, the way you do," he said.

"Why not?" she asked.

"Because of our enhanced senses," he said. "Especially where a mate is concerned."

Oh, God, he didn't really mean emotions.

He meant arousal.

"So you can tell when I'm thinking about…" she trailed off, really, really not wanting to say *sex*.

He nodded.

"If it makes you feel any better, I can't stop thinking about it either."

She felt the blood rush to her cheeks.

"That is how it must be, my love," he said, stopping to take her hands. "It is right that I crave you. You are the sun to my moon, the light to my darkness. Our joining will move the heavens."

Atlas chose that moment to wake up and whimper in her arms.

"Oh dear," he said. "Poor little fellow, he has had a busy day."

"I can't believe the sun is setting already," Phoebe said, gazing at the pink sky.

"The days here are short," he replied. "We should hurry if we want to secure everything before dark."

"Of course," she said. "And Atlas needs his feeding."

They continued walking until the docks came into sight. The pink sunset reflecting on the water lent them a surreal glow that was quite beautiful.

But Phoebe couldn't enjoy the view.

Beside her, Tyro seemed to be growing more tense the closer they drew toward home.

She didn't dare ask, but she was certain she knew the reason. His amped up senses must have picked up on something unpleasant.

An intruder.

She only hoped she had hidden her trunk well enough to escape the notice of any uninvited guests.

10

PHOEBE

Phoebe's heart was pounding as they approached the yurt.

"Why don't I feed Atlas?" Tyro suggested.

She handed over the baby gratefully and dashed off to find her trunk.

Please let it be here. Please let it be here. Please let it be here.

She ran to the corner beside her bed, where she could see the outline of the trunk under the throw she had spread over it in an attempt to make it look like a bedside table.

It looked untouched.

She whisked off the throw to get access to the lock, feeling like she needed to peek inside, just to be sure.

Phoebe looked around, but there was no one but Tyro, who was focused on warming a cell of milk for the baby.

The lock was physical, with a biometric backup, so it would be nearly impossible for anyone else to open it without clear signs of damage. But still...

Phoebe pulled at the chain around her neck until she extracted the key at the end, and then unlocked the trunk using the key and her fingerprint at the same time.

Everything inside was just as she had left it.

She closed and relocked it quickly, dropping the key safely back down the front of her blouse.

"Everything okay?" Tyro called to her from the kitchen.

"Yes," she said. "But I need to lock this thing down before I can really feel better."

"I didn't want to scare you, but I scented someone on the docks on the way in," he said, confirming her suspicions. "Not in here though. Whoever it was must have been more interested in the farm than the personal stuff."

A chill went down Phoebe's spine. Other than the trunk, there was nothing personal she cared about more than the farm.

She straightened up and decided to do something that might help, or at the very least would keep her mind occupied until Tyro was ready to help secure her trunk.

She headed over to the droid, examining its control panel. If it could be programed for guard duty, that would be a life changer.

She slid it out of silent follow mode, figuring it might as well help her understand its own potential.

There was a muted hum and a few lights on the panel blinked. Then the droid opened its "eyes" - just two blue lights on the front screen. They weren't really necessary, but she knew the manufacturers gave droids features like that to make people more comfortable interacting with them.

"Hello, my lady," it said in a smooth, vaguely male voice.

"Hello," she replied. "Welcome to our home. I'm Phoebe, that man is Tyro, and the baby is called Atlas." She spoke slowly, knowing the droid would need to calibrate to the slight differences in accent and pitch of her voice, compared to its last renter.

Tyro looked over at her, brows slightly raised.

"Hello, Phoebe, Tyro and Atlas," the droid replied politely.

"What do you like to be called?" Phoebe asked.

The droid "blinked" its eyes. "No one has ever asked me that question. I am a Quality 4T Household Droid, manufactured in the Saylin Prefecture."

"How about we call you Saylin?" Phoebe offered.

"I would like that," it replied.

"Saylin, what can you do?" she asked.

"That is a question best answered by my manual, available online day or night at the following address—" it began.

"Wait, Saylin," she said quickly. "I know I can look up a list. But what do you do best? What do most people have you do?"

"Many users have found that I am effective at carrying goods while they are shopping," Saylin replied. "I often assist in the kitchen with food preparation and cooking. I can watch over younglings, like your own small one, and assist with cleaning and finding lost objects."

"Can you perform guard duty?" she asked.

"I am not a battle droid," he replied.

"You say that you watch over younglings," she replied. "What do you do when they get into trouble?"

"If the youngling gets into mischief, I am programmed to give one of several thousand approved speeches, based on the mischief at hand," the droid explained.

"What if the youngling won't listen to the speech?" she asked.

"I alert the parents," Saylin said. "Is your youngling a troublemaker?"

"How do you alert the parents?" she asked.

"In whatever manner they prefer," Saylin said. "Usually a sort of a siren sound is most effective."

"What would you do if a stranger approached a youngling you were minding?" Phoebe asked.

In the kitchen, Tyro had stopped preparing the milk to listen.

"I would announce to the stranger that they must not come closer," Saylin said. "Then I would sound my alarm to the parents."

"That's excellent," Phoebe said. "I'm going to ask you for an alternate option to your programming. Do you have enough memory to program another chain, similar to that one?"

"Yes, Phoebe," the droid said.

"I would like you to consider this dock farm and our yurt to be like a second youngling," Phoebe said. "If a stranger approaches, you will ask them to leave, and you will alert Tyro and me."

The droid blinked and whirred for a moment.

"It is done," the droid said. "I have never acted as a guard droid before. This is clever coding, but it may have weaknesses we have not anticipated. I apologize in advance for my inexperience and hope that I may serve to your satisfaction."

"Saylin, I thank you for your earnest efforts," Phoebe said. "Solving problems together in ways we couldn't alone is why I love working with droids, like you. I want you to know that I will never be angry if my coding doesn't work. And I hope you will be honest with me if you anticipate problems with something I ask you to do."

"Phoebe," the droid said at once, "I anticipate a problem."

"Excellent," she said. "What is it?"

"From my current position I am unable to see if any strangers are approaching the dock," the droid said. "Also, I do not have a complete list of non-strangers."

"Thank you for your astute observations," Phoebe said. "Most times when I want you to watch over the dock it will be because Tyro and I are sleeping, or away from the farm. Right now, it's okay that you can't see enough to help with this task."

"I see," the droid said.

"And for now, Tyro, Atlas and myself are the only non-strangers," she said. "We are new to this place. But we hope in time there will be many more non-strangers."

"Excellent, my lady," the droid said.

"Can you tell me what kind of maintenance would be best for you right now?" she asked.

"My major maintenance is complete," the droid replied. "I will prepare a list of minor servicing that might help me serve you better."

"Thank you," Phoebe replied. "I will be sure to attend to you in the morning, unless there is something more urgently needed."

"No, my lady," Saylin replied.

"Excellent," Phoebe said. "I am very glad you have joined our home, Saylin."

She headed for the kitchen, very pleased with her choice of droids. This one was very quick on its feet.

"That was incredible," Tyro said, handing her a plate of something that looked like bread and butter.

"I grew up on a farm with a droid work force," she said. "We got very lucky with Saylin. He's a keeper."

"You're so gentle with him," Tyro said. "Most people treat them like tools or just machines, no different than a pump impeller."

"My daddy always said that it was important to treat our workers politely, whether they were organic or manufactured. He said you could tell a lot about a person by how they treated others when there was no personal gain involved," Phoebe said fondly. "He was always kind to our droids. They understand us very well, and the relationship is always better when we are honest with them and they can trust us. Saylin could save our lives one day with his own ingenuity. But he won't take independent action unless we make sure he knows we want him to pipe up if we're making a mistake."

"Isn't that dangerous?" Tyro asked.

"How so?"

"What if you have just given him the freedom to do something against our interests?" Tyro asked.

"He would never do anything against our interests, would you, Saylin?" Phoebe replied indignantly.

"Of course not, my lady," the droid replied instantly.

"His interest is in serving ours," she said. "That is how he is programmed. The knowledge of his unparalleled service gives him pleasure."

"Indeed, my lady understands me well," Saylin said. "The small freedom she offers will allow me to augment my service to your home."

"It's important that we talked about it though, because someone else might consider being corrected by a droid to be an impertinence," she told Tyro. "Communication is the most important part of our relationship."

Atlas had finished his milk and let out a loud burp.

"Someone was hungry," she said.

Atlas wiggled his little green fingers at her.

She took him in her arms, relishing his warm weight.

"*Mah,*" he said, leaning forward until his forehead touched hers.

"Did he just call you mama?" Tyro asked in wonder.

"No, I'm pretty sure it's just baby talk," she replied. But her own heart had surged with love at the sound. "He'll know our names soon enough."

"My lady, may I warm your meal?" Saylin offered.

"No thank you," she said. "But there's something you can do for us. Once Atlas falls asleep, we'll ask you to watch over him while we go out to check on the farm."

"I can watch over him now, my lady, if you place him in his cradle," Saylin offered. "I am programmed with many songs, stories and even light displays to help younglings feel peaceful for sleeping."

Phoebe glanced down at Atlas.

He did look sleepy.

"Do you want Saylin to sing you songs?" she asked him softly.

She placed him gently in his cradle.

As soon as he began to protest, Saylin rolled over to him, a spectrum, of light colors glowing alternately on his front screen and soft, silly music playing from his main speaker.

Atlas stopped whimpering immediately and squeaked at the droid, waving his little hands.

"Hello, young one," Saylin said politely. "Let's have some resting music."

Phoebe watched for a few minutes as the droid eased the baby into a state of peacefulness with a sweet melody, accompanied by soft, dancing lights on his front screen.

"Okay," she told Tyro. "Come on."

11

TYRO

Tyro stepped out of the yurt and looked around.

Though he knew already that someone had been here while they were away, he was sure that no one was around currently.

He moved aside once he was convinced it was safe, allowing Phoebe to join him.

She smiled as the breeze lifted her golden hair.

He smiled back, almost in pain from the delicious scent of her.

"So you think someone was here earlier?" she asked.

"I know it," he said.

They walked quietly to the end of the dock to survey the scene.

The pump was just as they had left it, thankfully. With the new impeller, he hoped to be able to get it up and running tomorrow. The toolboxes all seemed to be intact, the netting was all undamaged, and so was the pulley system.

"What's wrong?" Phoebe asked.

"Nothing," he replied. "That's the trouble. Who would come here and not touch anything?"

She didn't answer, because there was no answer to that.

He leaned over the dock to look at the luxberries themselves.

"Oh," he said, sighing as he spotted the problem.

"What?" she asked.

"There's a hole in the containment fence," he told her.

"Would the berries… get away?" she asked, quirking an eyebrow.

"No," he said. "But the lake is full of animals that would love to eat the berries or damage the farm in other ways. We need to repair the fence right away."

"There are animals in there?" she asked, wrinkling her nose.

"Yes," he chuckled. "Don't worry, you don't have to go down there. I can take care of it."

"Like hell," she retorted. "I'm a farmer, and a farmer isn't afraid to get her hands dirty. A real farmer would never ask a hand to do something she can't do herself."

"So I'm your hand now?" he teased.

In reality he was delighted. This was exactly the proper attitude for a farmer on a frontier moon. He only hoped she was a good swimmer. If so, she would take this moon by storm.

To his surprise, and further delight, she began removing her clothing.

"What are you doing?" he asked.

"My farm is in danger," she said simply, looking at him like he was crazy. "I'm going to swim down there and protect it. My extra clothing will just weigh me down."

Her hands were at the hem of her shift and she was clearly about to pull it over her head.

He wanted nothing more than to let her, and then feast on the view of her luminous flesh in the pink twilight. But he knew that wasn't really an option.

"Phoebe," he sighed. "Your motivation is admirable. But the animals in the water are extremely dangerous. The only way to swim in this lake is to wear water armor."

"Do I have water armor?" she asked, her eyes wide.

He led her to the locked box where her armor was kept.

"You do," he told her as he lifted it out and handed it to her.

"What about you?" she asked. "Do you know how to swim?"

"I'm a green dragon," he said. "What do you think?"

"Is that supposed to mean something to me?" she asked, sliding the armor over her legs.

To most people, one dragon was pretty much the same as every other. But Tyro knew that was far from the truth.

"Dragons have different abilities, and you can guess at some of them if you know our colorations," he explained. "As a green dragon, long distance swimming is part of my skillset."

"Well that's going to be handy," she said. "You must have been jazzed that your baby was assigned to a submerged farm."

"I was," he said quietly. "Until I saw how unhappy it made you."

She looked up at him, something like pain in her dark eyes.

"Are you okay?" he asked her.

She nodded, getting back to the task of donning her suit.

"Where's your armor?"

"I don't need it," he said, helping her get the final pieces in place. "Benefit of being a dragon. Now we just need our tool set."

Together they went through the tools on the dock and selected the right ones to repair the fence.

"Ready?" he asked her.

She nodded.

"If you get into trouble, just touch the silver button at your wrist," he told her. "It will set off a signal that will alert me immediately."

"Okay," she told him, checking out the button.

He turned to the lake.

It had been so long since he'd had a chance to swim. The ocean back on Ignis-7 seemed like a distant memory.

He dove in and let the water embrace him as it always did.

Instantly, he could feel the life in each drop, the quiver of other creatures below, and the breath of the plant life purifying the lake.

He resurfaced and held his arms out to Phoebe. She jumped without hesitation.

Time seemed to stand still as she moved toward him, her hair lifting from her shoulders in a glossy swirl, her eyes sparkling.

Then she landed in his arms in the water with a huge splash.

He pulled her close without meaning to, pressing his lips to the top of her head.

She snuggled closer, maddening him with her sweet scent.

"Let's fix this fence," she whispered.

He nearly groaned, but she was right, of course. The sooner they fixed the fence, the closer they were to a running farm.

He dove under the surface again and she joined him there, her hair a golden cloud around her. Moving slowly and carefully, he crimped each bit of the fence back into its proper shape.

After a moment she swam back up to the surface.

He was worried, but she was back again before he could check on her.

She must have been getting another breath. He had forgotten how little time these creatures could spend underwater.

She put her hand out for the tool and he handed it over and was impressed to see her following exactly what he had done before.

The fencing was lightweight but strong. It took strength and coordination to reshape it. Phoebe was obviously good with her hands.

He tried not to think of what other things those skilled hands might be good at.

They continued their work, each stage punctuated by Phoebe's comings and goings for air.

At last, the fence was in one piece again.

He held his finger out to her to caution against touching the fencing.

She nodded.

He slid his finger against the sensor in a pattern and the fence electrified again.

He took Phoebe's hand and they surfaced together. She filled her lungs once more before speaking.

"So the fence is charged?" she asked.

"Not enough to harm anyone," he explained. "Just enough to make it unpleasant for fish to try to sneak inside and eat the berries."

The sky above was darkening to a deep blue, except

along the fiery horizon. Clotho was still, as if holding its breath at the midway point between day and night.

"Do we have time to check out the rest of the farm?" Phoebe asked.

"Of course," he told her. "But let me lend you my breath this time."

"Lend me your breath?" she echoed.

"It won't sustain you forever underwater, but it will allow you to explore a little longer," he told her.

"How do we do it?" she asked.

Gods love her eagerness, he wanted to lend her everything he had.

"Come close," he told her. "This will be like a kiss."

She moved to him quickly, tilting her head back like the leading lady in a hologram picture.

He bent and placed his lips on hers.

Sensations washed over his body, as if his life were flashing before him. But it was the future and not the past. The two of them were laughing on a picnic blanket as Atlas took his first steps. Her belly was full with a second child. He held her close under a thick fur, making love to her silently before the fire as the children slept.

It was a dream, he knew that. But he could make it real, if he didn't push her too fast.

Phoebe whimpered and he swallowed up the sound as well as the rest of the air in her lungs.

Her hands tightened on his arms.

He filled her with a breath of his own.

She froze at the sensation, which must have been very strange to her. He could feel her body tremble as he pulled back slightly.

"Are you okay?" he asked.

"Yes," she whispered. "I'm a bit light headed, but that's going away."

"I've basically oversaturated your blood with oxygen," he told her. "You won't crave a breath for a long time now."

"Like a hippo," she said in a wondrous voice.

"What?" he asked.

"On old Earth, there was a creature called a hippopotamus. Children loved seeing them in the zoo and reading picture books about them, though the creatures were viciously territorial and dangerous in the wild. Hippos spend their time under water, but have to come up to take a breath every half hour or so."

"That's amazing," he told her. "I wish I could see a picture of one."

"I'll draw one for you when we get home," she told him, warming his heart by calling the yurt their home.

"Are you ready to go under water and try it out?" he asked.

"Very ready," she told him.

"We'll just take a quick swim around the berries and then go back," he said.

She took his hand and they dove under the surface together.

The lake was murky, murkier than it should be for ideal farming. He was glad they had the parts ready to get the pump up and running.

He could barely see Phoebe if she wasn't right beside him. And it was getting dark outside, which meant that soon she would have a wonderful surprise.

He fixed his eyes on her lovely face.

She was clearly enjoying the time underwater without craving air. He wished he had done it sooner. They could have worked more efficiently on the fence if she had not needed to surface for air so many times. But he hadn't been sure if she would accept his gift so eagerly when they were still on the dock. Something about the calmness of the water had seemed to relax her a bit.

He led her along the fence line so she could see the many thousands of berries that already grew in her submerged garden.

Soon they would have even more. His mate was smart and motivated. A year from tonight, the farm would be exponentially larger. He had no doubt.

Tyro watched, and he saw the exact moment when she noticed the luxberries.

Her face went soft with wonder and then her dark eyes met his and she smiled, squeezing his hand in a way that made him warm all over.

The luxberries were glowing.

Their soft light made him think of candlelight. It was romantic, even here in the cool depths of the murky water.

He reached out slowly to stroke her cheek.

She closed her eyes and leaned into his touch, and his heart was full to bursting.

She opened her eyes and pointed upward.

To Tyro, it felt like they had been underwater for a heartbeat. But it had clearly been longer if Phoebe needed a breath.

12

PHOEBE

Phoebe shivered as they crawled out of the water and onto the dock and the cool air hit her wet skin.

All around the dock the berries glowed like tiny stars captured in the water, almost like a reflection of the starry sky above.

"You're cold," Tyro said. "Come to me."

She moved to him without thinking, and when he lifted her into his arms, she relaxed against his chest like it was the most natural thing in the world.

"They're so beautiful. Why do they glow?" she asked. "Is it bioluminescence?"

"In a way," he told her. "The berries have a symbiotic relationship with a harmless bacteria common to this lake. The bacteria that makes the berries glow."

"But you're supposed to eat them?" she asked.

"They're delicious," he told her. "Very similar to Terran grapes, but lighter and crisper. But it's the glow that makes them so coveted. Luxberries are used on wedding cakes, in very high-end party drinks, and for other evening occasions where they can impress people."

"Amazing," Phoebe said. "It's going to be more like camellia farming than I would have thought."

"How so?" he asked.

"When a crop is prized for its beauty rather than its size or quantity, farming it requires a certain amount of patience," she explained. "That's something I'm used to. It makes me feel better to have a handle on the mindset, even if I'll be learning everything else from scratch."

"It won't take you long to learn everything else," Tyro predicted. "You are extremely sharp and hard working. This farm will be very productive."

"I hope so," she said. "I want to give Atlas an amazing life. I want him to be proud of the farm."

Tyro pressed his lips to her forehead.

She felt the sizzle of attraction and a warm feeling of acceptance. She closed her eyes as he carried her back to the yurt.

When Tyro opened the door, baby Atlas was sleeping in his cradle with Saylin watching over him intently.

"Thank you, Saylin," Phoebe said.

"It was my pleasure, my lady," the droid replied in a low tone. "I will now stand duty over my second youngling, the farm."

"Good work," Tyro said.

Phoebe smiled against his chest. He was making an effort to treat the droid with kindness and respect. He had listened to her earlier.

"Thank you, my lord," Saylin said as he rolled outside to stand guard.

Suddenly, the yurt seemed so peaceful, their privacy so fraught with possibility.

Tyro placed Phoebe gently on the floor.

She gazed up at him and then giggled.

"What is it?" he asked.

"We're so gross," she replied, glancing down at her suit. "Look at all the muck from the lake."

"Fortunately, that is a problem with an easy solution," Tyro told her. "Come."

He headed for the bathroom and she followed, her blood heating at the thought of what was to come.

He closed the door behind them and stepped closer to her.

Phoebe held her breath and locked eyes with the big green warrior as he slid his finger down the magnetic clasp of her suit, releasing it.

He slowly peeled the sleeves from her arms, removing the suit and the shift beneath, then sliding her undergarments off.

He straightened and she could hear his breathing was faster now. She swore she could sense the heavy pound of his heart.

He offered her his hand and helped her step out of the pile of clothing.

"Shower on," he said softly.

The water began to flow from the showerhead on the ceiling.

She watched as he carefully attended to her suit and clothing, hanging it on a bar on the far wall when he was finished.

She tried not to stare openly when he began stripping away his own clothes, but it was impossible not to look.

The enormous warrior was bristling with muscles and his thick cock twitched when she gazed at it.

"Gods, woman," he murmured.

She stepped into the warm spray of water, luxuriating in the heat returning to her body.

She closed her eyes and let the water stream down her face and hair.

When she opened them again, Tyro was beside her, pouring an amber liquid into his huge palm.

"I will tend to you," he told her.

She nodded, feeling weak-kneed.

Phoebe had never been naked with a man before. But somehow, the idea of allowing him to do something as intimate as wash her hair felt infinitely more intense.

She closed her eyes again as he massaged her scalp, his big fingers kneading and soothing as he worked the bubbles into a thick lather.

"Rinse," he murmured.

She leaned back into the warm spray, moaning with pleasure as he massaged the soap out of her hair.

He made a growling sound in the back of his throat that rumbled inside her.

Phoebe opened her eyes.

"I'm sorry," he said immediately. "My dragon longs for you when you make that sound. It is not an easy longing to control."

A wave of need washed over her, sending her senses spiraling so that she couldn't answer. He poured more of the liquid into his palm and smoothed it down her arms, across her chest.

She closed her eyes and waited for him to touch her breasts. They ached for him, as if suddenly she had twice as many nerve endings.

When his thumbs brushed her nipples, she cried out again.

He froze and took a deep breath, then continued to slide his soapy hands all over her breasts, her belly, her hips.

Phoebe felt the rough callouses of his hands and the silky smoothness of the soap. She could smell the musky, woodsy scent that was all Tyro, mixed with the crisp soapy smell. He hummed out encouragement as she moved into his hands, and the deep sound sent more vibrations through her, making her ache all over for more, more, more.

When he moved his hand between her legs she clung to his shoulders, helplessly lifting her hips to encourage him.

"Phoebe, oh, Phoebe," he intoned as his fingers slid against her swollen sex.

He pulled away too soon, leaving her frantic.

"Soon, my love," he crooned. "Help me bathe and I will take you to bed and pleasure you properly."

He poured the soap into her palm and she went up on her toes to reach his hair. Even then he had to bend down to allow her to work the suds into his tangled mane.

She worked her way down the solid planes of his chest and his ridged abs. He held his breath as she went lower, soaping his hips, his thighs and calves, and working her way back up.

His cock was stiff and swollen. Phoebe had never seen one up close like this, and she was fascinated. It didn't seem possible that it was meant to fit inside her.

She slid a soapy finger gently from the base up to the head.

Tyro groaned and his hands clenched into fists at his side.

Encouraged, she wrapped her hand around him and slid her hand up and down once.

He stiffened and twitched in her hand and she felt her own body respond.

What would it be like for him to be inside me?

The idea was intoxicating instead of frightening.

She slid her hand up and down again, trying to memorize the sounds he made, the expression on his beautiful face of pleasure and pain mixed together.

"Enough," he said suddenly, grasping her wrist and pulling her off him.

She watched as he rinsed the soap from his body, rivulets of water releasing the pale bubbles and revealing the verdant tone of his flesh to her once more.

When he was finished, he lifted her in his arms.

"Shower off," he said.

Instantly, the water ceased flowing and he was carrying her into the bedroom, placing her in bed, crawling into the covers with her.

She reached for him, needing to feel him close, his skin against hers, hearts pounding in rhythm.

"Phoebe, I need to claim you," he told her, his deep voice almost choked with desire.

"Yes," she whispered back.

"But you must know that this is forever, my love," he told her. "You are mine, and I am yours. Always. Will you accept me as your mate?"

"Yes," she moaned.

"I will make you ready," he murmured.

She closed her eyes as he fed on her breasts. His hot mouth was so clever, sending her into spirals of passion, even as she wished he would just take her.

But the big warrior seemed determined to take his time.

He brushed his lips against her belly, then nuzzled her thighs.

She pressed them together, uncertain.

"Please," he groaned. "I need to taste you."

"I never... no one has ever..." she couldn't find the words to tell him.

"*Good*," he told her, gazing into her eyes.

She relaxed and allowed him to kiss her inner thighs, his breath hot against the tender flesh.

Waves of need and anticipation washed over her.

When his lips brushed her sex at last, she moaned, uncertain whether it was relief or frustration she felt.

He groaned as he inhaled her scent and then pressed his mouth to her, licking and suckling lightly, sending her into a frenzy of need.

Phoebe cried out, her whole body shivering for the climax he was bringing on with every lazy movement of his cruel mouth.

She moaned and wailed as he slowly brought her closer and closer to the edge of the abyss.

At last, he pressed one thick finger against her opening, flicking her little pearl with his tongue as he eased it inside.

Phoebe floated for a delirious instant, then the pleasure crashed down on her and she was soaring.

Tyro's moan against her sex pushed her higher and higher until at last, the pleasure slowed.

He crawled up to her, pinning her still throbbing body to the bed with his hips. His cock throbbed against her belly and his mouth shimmered with her moisture.

She was ready for him, so ready.

"Mine," he growled.

"Yours," she agreed, wrapping her legs around his hips, eager to seal their bond.

He took himself in his hand and slid the tip of his cock against her.

The pleasure of it was blinding. She felt ready to climax again almost instantly.

Suddenly, there was an unbearably loud klaxon sound coming from outside, piercing her thoughts and breaking the spell.

It was loud, high-pitched and unmistakable.

The droid was announcing the presence of danger.

13

TYRO

Tyro fought the urge to scream.

He was here, at the gates of heaven, his Phoebe warm and wanting pinned under him.

The dragon roared in frustration in his chest.

But his need to protect her was greater than his need to claim her.

He leapt out of bed and landed in a crouch, the change already wavering the air around him.

"Tyro?" Phoebe murmured from the bed.

But he could not answer, his whole body was wrapped up in the shift. He had to get out of the yurt before his wings unfurled.

He made it out the door and onto the dock before the radiant wings exploded out of his shoulder blades and the scales slid up from his forearms to cover him.

He rose from the dock on wings of green light, hovering just high enough not to strain the structure with his weight.

The droid had rolled to the end of the dock and was facing off with someone.

Tyro roared, the dragon at the forefront of his consciousness now.

In the background, the man urged the beast to be thoughtful and deliberate.

The dragon begrudgingly obeyed.

They were close enough now to make out the figure on the dock. He was an older man, wearing the kind of lake armor that came cheaply in pieces. It was not as effective as full armor, and this set was mismatched and worn.

The man shivered, eyes wide with fear that Tyro could smell thick on the air.

There was a click behind him.

Mate.

He spun on her, furious that she would come out into the open.

His first instinct was fear for her safety.

His second was the memory that she was readied for claiming.

He could not allow her to be in the presence of another male.

The dragon was roaring at her before the man in the back of his mind could stop him.

"Back off," she yelled right back at him, unafraid. "This is my farm and my family. If something threatens it, I have every right to be here."

The dragon snorted his dissent.

"Yes, I do," she insisted, striding right up to him and poking his scaly chest. "If you don't like it, I'm sorry, but you have to deal with it."

He snorted again, but this time it was a resigned sound.

She had called his bluff.

She was his mate, he would protect her from anything

happening out here. She did not have to cower in the yurt if that was not her wish.

"Go back and watch over Atlas, please, Saylin," Phoebe said to the droid. "And thank you for your service on the dock tonight. We are very fortunate that you were here and ready to spring into action."

"My pleasure, my lady," the droid said. The whirring and buzzing sounds he made as he rolled back to tend to the baby somehow managed to sound gratified.

"I've used our comms to notify the authorities," Phoebe said to the frightened man in a calm, clear voice. "We will wait here until they come."

He nodded, not taking his eyes off Tyro.

"Tyro, maybe you could shift back for a minute," Phoebe suggested. "This man knows what you are capable of now. But he might be more likely to explain why he's sabotaging us if he isn't afraid you're going to eat him."

She held up a tunic for him that she must have grabbed on her way out.

Eat him, indeed.

The dragon was indignant. Did she not know that the great green dragons were herbivores?

The man in the back of his head was grateful that she had covered herself before emerging, and had even thought of his need for clothing.

He closed his eyes and soon was standing in his man form.

"Who are you," Phoebe asked the man in a non-threatening tone. "And why did you come here tonight?"

That was probably the wrong question, it was far too open-ended. But he listened anyway as he pulled on his breeches. This mate of his had a way of getting people to do what she wanted.

"I'm Guckett. I run the patch two farms down," the man replied proudly. "I was hoping there was something here I could use, or sell."

"I respect your honesty," Phoebe said. "Things must be hard on this moon."

"For some of us, they are," he said, giving the dock a significant look.

"Yes, I've got a nice set-up," Phoebe told him. "But it all belongs to the baby in there. Part of what was required of me when I adopted him was that I work this farm and give him a good life, since he began it with nothing."

"The child is a foundling?" the man asked, his voice less harsh.

"Yes," she said. "But I'm his mother now and no one can change that, no matter how they may steal from him and wish ill on us."

Tyro watched in amazement as the man hung his head in shame.

"Things are hard, as you say, miss," the man said. "My own children are doing without these days."

"I'm very sorry to hear that," Phoebe said.

"The lake is polluted," he told her. "Too many began trying to farm at once. The water is thick with bacteria and who knows what else."

"Do you have a pump?" she asked.

"Broke down," he said quietly.

"Tyro would be glad to look at it for you," she said, acknowledging her mate's presence for the first time. "We can come by whenever you like."

"I don't have the parts," he said. "Can't afford 'em."

"We'll get them for you," she offered. "It's not a problem."

Suddenly the man straightened and a hard look was in his eyes again.

"I'll take no charity," he said stiffly.

"I didn't mean it as charity," she told him quickly. "We're neighbors. We should help each other."

But he crossed his arms in front of his skinny chest, and even refused her offer of a blanket to warm him.

"Listen, I'm not going to press charges," she said wearily. "But will you talk with the other neighbors? Let them know we're not trying to hurt anyone?"

He opened his mouth to answer but the sound of a siren drowned out whatever he had been going to say.

Tyro spun on his heel to see the droid with the baby in his arms, sounding the alarm once more, because the police had arrived.

14

PHOEBE

Phoebe sighed.

She had really hoped she could send the poor man away before the police arrived, or at least that the response would be somewhat subdued.

Instead, the officers were storming onto the dock, the determined droid rolling after them as if he meant to stop them.

There was one stocky officer and another one, tall and thin with some kind of hairless wolf on a leash.

She shuddered at the sight of it.

"Saylin, it's okay," she called to the droid. "Well done."

Instantly, he abandoned his defense and rolled back into the yurt with little Atlas.

"Are you the owner of this dock?" the stockier man asked Tyro in a loud voice.

"She is," Tyro said, pointing to Phoebe.

"What seems to be the trouble, madam?" His voice had gone saccharine-sweet, as if he thought she was a child who had gotten lost at a prefecture fair, or might have accidentally called the police instead of the food delivery service.

"We thought there was a prowler," she said carefully. "But it was only a neighbor coming to check on us."

The neighbor's eyes went wide with surprise. Then he nodded once.

"Why would he check on you in the middle of the night?" the deputy asked suspiciously.

"We've had some things happen," Phoebe said. "Vandalism, a part stolen from our pump."

"I'm sorry to hear that," the deputy said in a sly way. "Maybe we can do some extra patrolling, help you out. We'd be glad to extend you some extra protection."

Phoebe wasn't born yesterday. That meant he wanted a bribe. But she wasn't sure if that was an acceptable part of local custom, or if the man was just trying to take advantage of her apparent means.

Tyro shook his head almost imperceptibly.

"Oh, we'll be just fine," Phoebe said. "We have good neighbors and I know we'll all keep an eye out for each other. Can I fix you officers a cup of something warm to take with you?"

"Nah," the deputy said, looking disappointed. "Be careful now, keep an eye out. There's a lot of undesirables on this moon."

That much was clear. Phoebe resisted the impulse to roll her eyes.

Instead, she waved to the officers.

When they were nearly off the dock she turned back to her neighbor. But he was gone, leaving nothing but some quickly drying footprints behind to show he had ever been there.

"You were amazing," Tyro said softly. "I can't believe how well you handled that."

"We need friends," she said simply. "And Atlas needs a

community around him. Besides, it's not right that these people are suffering."

"I wish he would let us help," Tyro said thoughtfully.

"Maybe there's something we can do," Phoebe said.

"What did you have in mind?" he asked.

An idea began to form in her mind. But it was kind of far-fetched.

"We'll think of something," she said, not wanting to share it just yet.

"I'm sure we will," Tyro told her.

Suddenly, the memory of what they had been about to do came back to her.

"I'm sorry we were interrupted," she said.

"We'll try again tonight," he told her with a grin that set her blood rushing all over again. "For now, we have to get ready to start our day."

"*Tonight*?" she asked, wondering what he meant by that. It was already nighttime.

"Look at the sky," he whispered.

Sure enough, the sun was already rising again, casting a pink glaze over the lake. Morning had snuck up on them while they were dealing with the intruder and the police response.

"The nights are short here, but so are the days," he reminded her. "And we have much to do."

Just then the door to the yurt opened, releasing the wailing sounds of a hungry baby.

"We're coming, Saylin," Tyro called to the droid.

She allowed him to take her hand and they headed back to the yurt together.

Her mind was already distracted with the problem of their struggling neighbors. Her idea was ridiculous, but she really couldn't think of a better one.

Phoebe's father had always told her that sometimes the best way to come up with a solution was to ignore the problem for a while and let your mind work in its own time.

Maybe if she concentrated on the tasks that needed tending on her own farm, something better would come to her.

15

TYRO

Tyro hummed to himself as he unreeled the spool of hosing for the luxberry circulation system and Phoebe monitored the line for kinks or damage.

It was a beautiful day to spend with his beautiful mate. The sun was high in the sky and the breeze was cool and fragrant. They had eaten a hearty breakfast and Atlas was spending a happy time being told stories by the droid.

But he could tell Phoebe wasn't herself.

Something was troubling his mate, and Tyro thought it would eat him alive if he couldn't find some way to ease her worry.

She is frightened, his dragon whispered. *There are prowlers on the docks, and even the police force can't be trusted. Claim her. Make her feel safe under the promise of our protection.*

The idea was intoxicating, but Tyro would not grab her in the middle of the day and drag her down the dock. He would not claim her in front of the droid and child.

The dragon chuckled in his mind. It had no such compunctions.

Claim her. It is all she craves.

But Tyro wasn't so sure about that.

He could taste her longing in the air every time she was near, but there was something else too - a puzzle she was trying to solve.

"There," she called to him. "That's all."

He dove into the cool water, laying out the hose around the berries as best he could.

While they might have better equipment than most of the farmers on the lake, their setup was still less than ideal. He wished they had twice as much hosing, and a bigger pump too.

The neighbor was right about the quality of the murky water among the berries. They could run the pump day and night and he still wasn't sure it would clear.

He emerged and pulled himself onto the dock.

For a moment, Phoebe gazed in open admiration at his dripping form.

His dragon preened and purred in his chest.

Then the furrow reappeared on her brow and he knew she was deep in thought once more.

"Is that all we have?" she asked him.

"Yes," he told her. "That was the last hose. Nothing to do now but let the water circulate for a while. We'll get the pump going tomorrow and hopefully the water will clear up quickly."

She nodded.

"It's going to be dark again soon," he said. "We should get inside to clean up, and then eat something."

His words hung in the air, his unspoken question outstanding.

Will you still accept my claim?

The alternative was unthinkable. He had never lacked

confidence in anything. The whisper of doubt made him feel as if his soul were splitting in two.

But Tyro wanted to make her happy. He did not want to see her torn in this way.

They walked down the dock and he held the door open to the yurt for her.

"Hello, Saylin," she said. "Hello Atlas."

Her voice sounded happier as she greeted them, and Tyro felt a touch of relief.

"Oh no," she said, looking at the counter.

He followed her gaze.

The camellia plant she had brought with her was wilting in earnest.

"I'm sorry, Phoebe," he told her. "Perhaps it needs more sun after all."

"It's not meant for this climate," she said, shaking her head. "I don't know why I brought it here."

He studied the once-shining green leaves and the deflated blossom. She was right, it was a hothouse flower, too delicate for a moon like Clotho.

Not unlike Phoebe herself.

He might claim her and even protect her, but she had been raised in gentler circumstances.

Could he really expect her to thrive on this frontier land with him?

Was it fair for him to bind her to his beast, when it was his duty to stay here with the child no matter what?

The dragon roared its frustration in his chest, but Tyro blocked out the sound.

I have to think. I have to make the right choice for the woman I love.

16

TYRO

As night fell, Tyro sat back in his chair, feeling better after a nourishing meal.

Phoebe held Atlas in her arms and smiled down at his sweet, dimpled face.

Tyro could hardly blame her. The child was perfect, down to the last hair on his head.

"Thank you for cooking," Phoebe said.

"It was my pleasure," he told her honestly. "I know you need time to bond with the baby."

"He's amazing," Phoebe said, reaching out a tentative hand to stroke Atlas's fluffy hair.

Atlas laughed and kicked his little feet.

"What's so funny about that?" she asked, lifting him up and blowing air against his small belly, creating a large, undignified sound.

Atlas shrieked with laughter.

"What was that?" Tyro asked her, amazed. "How did you know he would like that?"

"I'm not sure it has a technical term, but my daddy

called that a zurburt," she said. "Kids love the noise, and also it tickles. It's kind of the total package."

"I will remember it," Tyro told her. "Terrans are high-spirited."

"Sometimes," she said, shrugging. "We can be moody too."

"So your literature would suggest," he agreed.

She smiled at that and he saw the warmth in her eyes again, the warmth that had been missing all day.

"Listen," she said. "I'd really like to explore the lake."

"Of course," he replied. "I'm sure Saylin can watch Atlas while we explore."

"I meant, by myself," she said gently. "Sometimes I like a little alone time. It helps me think."

"Oh," he replied, surprised and a little saddened.

Tyro had never wished to do anything alone in his life. And right now, the mate bond crackled and hummed between them. Could she not feel it?

Maybe she felt it, but did not want it anymore.

The dragon roared in pain. *Who will protect her?*

"Phoebe, it's dark again, and I'm a little worried about you being out there alone at night," he said carefully. "We've already had some unwanted guests."

"I'll take the droid," she said, frowning. "And you know I'm a grown woman, right?"

He knew that all too well.

"My only wish is to protect you," he replied indignantly.

Atlas whimpered, and Phoebe wrapped her arms around him and pressed her lips to his dark locks.

"Don't worry, little one," she crooned. "I'll be back again in an hour, and we'll play some more."

"Stay close to shore," he warned. "There are things in the deep water that are far worse than any of our neighbors."

"I will," she assured him.

Tyro's heart ached, but he rose and cleared the dishes.

When he came back to the table, Phoebe was standing with Atlas.

"Here, I'll take him," Tyro said, putting his arms out.

She handed the child over and headed to the washroom to change into the lake armor.

Tyro worried about her, but he was also worried about himself. He had no idea how he was going to survive her night swim. He was already going out of his mind, and she hadn't even left yet.

By the time she got out of the bathroom he was pacing.

"See you in a bit," she told him.

She was out the door, with the droid in tow, before he could formulate an answer.

"Now what?" he asked the baby.

But Atlas did not answer, because he couldn't talk.

Tyro paced on, trying to drown out the dragon's agony long enough to come up with a plan.

After a few minutes, Atlas began to whimper.

"Oh, baby," Tyro said, feeling guilty. "Let's do something fun. Hey, we can have some beach time. How about that?"

Tyro liked this idea so much he immediately grabbed the bag he kept packed and ready for trips to the rocky beach. It was dark, but Atlas liked the beach at any time, and the fresh air would tire him out after his meal.

They headed out of the yurt and into the starry night. The sound of the lake lapping at the shore and the scent of distant wood fires soothed his senses slightly.

He spread out the blanket and sat down with Atlas, placing a few toys he had made for the boy beside him.

As usual, Atlas was more interested in Tyro than the toys. He squeaked at him, waving his little fingers around before snatching up a wooden rattle and gazing at it with wide eyes.

"This is why I'm here," Tyro said out loud, for his benefit more than Atlas's. "I'm here for you, sweet boy."

Guarding Atlas was the greatest honor of Tyro's life. It was selfish of him to fret over the mate bond, when his focus should be on the child.

Reluctantly, he let go of the tiny portion of him that just might have been out here to try to keep an eye on Phoebe.

She was right. She was an adult.

And as much as he craved her, she was not yet his mate.

The chubby little fellow on the blanket, on the other hand, was his charge.

Tyro vowed to remember that from here on in.

17

TYRO

Tyro was just settling in with Atlas, when an alarm pierced the air from the far side of the yurt.

"Not again," he groaned.

But there was no ignoring it. The whole lake would be up in arms if he didn't get to the droid and find out what was wrong.

"It's probably just another nosy neighbor," he grumbled to Atlas as he grabbed their things and jogged back to the dock, fighting the rising tide of panic in his chest.

Phoebe was out there alone.

What if she had really run into some sort of trouble?

He couldn't shift while carrying the little one, but he was nearly there anyway.

"What is it Saylin?" he called out.

But the droid did not stop sounding the alarm to explain.

By the time Tyro reached the yurt the dragon was flashing just under his skin, ready to be released as soon as he handed over the baby.

The scene when he turned the corner and reached the

far side of the yurt was the opposite of what he had imagined.

Images had flashed in Tyro's mind of a drowning Phoebe, of thieves, vandals, knives, blood, murky lake water, and every kind of foulness.

Instead, the droid was in all-out alarm mode over the approach of a well-dressed Terran man.

"Thank you, Saylin. That's enough," Tyro said.

Instantly, the droid stopped his alarm.

In the silence that followed, the man turned to Tyro and sniffed.

He was small, in the way of most Terrans when compared to the people of Ignis-7. His hair was pale, like Phoebe's, but more like thistle-corn than gold. His eyes were light too, in a way that made Tyro think of lizard-frog skin.

He wore clothing that made it clear he was not prepared to spend time on a frontier moon - doeskin shoes, and a woven shirt, and breeches that made him look like a Terran politician.

"I'm here for Phoebe," the man said in a bored voice.

"She's not here right now," Tyro said, remembering to control his temper as the dragon still simmered near the surface.

"I'll wait," the man said, looking at Tyro as if he expected him to drag out a chair and foot stool for him.

The dragon seethed in his chest at being treated like a servant, but Tyro managed to stay calm.

"Why do you want to see her?" he asked as politely as he could.

"Excuse me," the man said, in a disgusted tone, as if he didn't expect a hired guard to ask questions.

"I asked you why you're here," Tyro said again, calmly.

"Why don't you do your job and send the droid for her if

you aren't going to go yourself?" the man said. "You know you're very lucky she's so soft-hearted. I can't believe she let you bring your kid to work."

The dragon was rising up in Tyro's chest in spite of his best efforts to tamp it down. It wasn't too keen on the way this interloper was behaving. A drop into the lake from about a hundred meters up would probably help him remember his manners.

Footsteps behind him brought with them the deliriously alluring scent of his mate.

"Oh," she said suddenly as she turned the corner.

"Phoebe, do you know this man?" Tyro asked her.

"Of course she knows me," the man answered for her. "I'm her fiancé."

18

PHOEBE

Phoebe stood frozen on the dock, dripping and shocked.

"Phoebe?" Tyro murmured, turning to her. "Is this true?"

She opened her mouth and closed it again, completely at a loss for words.

Watching the pain transform his handsome face was like watching a fire consume an art museum. Her corresponding pain was visceral.

Cash doesn't love me. And I never loved him. He means so little to me that I never even thought to tell you...

But the words wouldn't come.

"I'll give you two some privacy," Tyro said, stalking down the dock.

"Would you like me to take the child?" Saylin piped up, rolling after him.

If Tyro leaves the baby here, he might never come back.

The terrifying idea was enough to rekindle Phoebe's power of speech.

"Tyro," she called to him.

But he merely handed over Atlas and kept walking.

"Phoebe, we need to talk." Cash's voice was annoyingly smooth.

But he was right.

"Fine," she said. "But I'm not going back with you. You should know that up front."

"Why don't you invite me in?" he suggested. "We can have a cup of tea and discuss things like civilized people."

She wavered. They really did need to talk. And doing it inside, over a cup of hot tea, sounded infinitely better than standing on a cold dock while she was soaking wet.

"I brought tea from home," he said, patting his pocket, which presumably held a pouch of her favorite flower tea. He might not love her, but he knew her well.

"Fine," she sighed. "But don't get any big ideas."

He nodded and gave her his signature half-smile.

That cute look might work on the widow Jones, but it will get you nowhere with me.

She headed inside and put the kettle on the warmer.

When she turned around, he had already closed the door behind him and sat at the kitchen counter. He pulled the pouch from his pocket and sure enough, the delicate scent of jasmine greeted her.

Phoebe prepared their cups and waited for the water to simmer.

"Your father misses you," Cash said, breaking the silence with the four words most capable of also breaking her heart.

"I miss him too," she admitted.

Cash nodded.

The kettle steamed and she pulled it off the warmer before it could boil, then slowly poured the water over the tea leaves in their mugs.

The scent brought back so many memories.

She closed her eyes and she could see the sun rising over the camellias, hear her father humming as he prepared their morning meal.

"Why did you run?" Cash asked quietly.

"I didn't want to get married," she said simply.

"Why not?" he asked.

"Can we be honest?"

"Your father spent thousands of credits on private detectives to track you down," he said. "I've been traveling for days to find this place. Honesty is exactly what I'm looking for."

"You came here just for answers?" she asked.

"And to bring you home," he said. "We need you back. Whatever I've done wrong, I'll fix it."

"How does the widow Jones feel about that?" she asked.

His eyes widened.

"You were only marrying me for my land," she said softly.

"And you were marrying me for my water," he said. "But I don't see that as a bad thing. It means we're alike."

"Both shallow, greedy fools," she muttered.

"No," he said, his lazy voice suddenly passionate. "The opposite of that. My farm has been in the family for generations. It's everything to me. And you feel the same way about yours. We belong to that land, Phoebe. Giving ourselves to protect it is an act of love, even if it's not for each other. Besides, we're young and attractive, developing those feelings over time would be practically inevitable between us. And if not, we'd find those pleasures elsewhere. But as long as we were together, our homes would be preserved and protected. Isn't that the most important thing?"

She stared at him in awe.

Though she had thought of him as foppish and foolish, he had just articulated all the same reasons she had been willing to marry him in the first place. She *did* love the land. She *was* willing to make sacrifices to protect her home. They shared values.

"And if marriage is out of the question, maybe we can work out something else," he added. "A means to share land and water without blending our families could be even better for both of us. A purely business relationship."

"Why didn't you offer me that instead of marriage in the first place?" she asked.

He sighed. "Promise you won't take this the wrong way?"

"Honesty is all I'm looking for," she echoed back at him with a wry smile.

He smiled back.

"Phoebe, you've always seemed so… proper and ladylike," he said carefully. "I thought you would *want* a marriage proposal rather than a business proposal. That way you could know you and your land would be cared for even when your father passed."

She bit her tongue, even though she wanted to scream at him. She had asked for honesty and he was giving it to her.

"But I know now that's not what you want," he said quickly. "Believe me. I can see you're super independent. You're out here running a submerged berry farm all by yourself, with nothing but some shoddy equipment, one droid and a body guard that brings his baby to work. I respect the hell out of that, Phoebe. And if you'll come home, I'd like to do business with you."

She smiled and nodded in acknowledgement. He understood her better after five minutes on this dock than he had after a lifetime as neighbors. Maybe he had a point.

"You need to be in a place where you belong, Phoebe," he said softly.

Suddenly she could hear the angry words of the people in the shop, see the scowl on the face of the man she'd caught on her dock. Everyone on this moon hated her.

"You're right," she said. "You're absolutely right."

19

TYRO

Tyro stalked away.

He had no plan, no destination, his feet merely carried him toward the village and farther from the woman who was tearing his soul into pieces.

I'm her fiancé.

She hadn't denied it.

And while things must have been complicated for her to leave her system and that man behind, it told Tyro two important things about Phoebe.

She hadn't trusted him enough to be honest with him about her past.

And she had run from another life once, a life with someone she cared about.

That man was everything Tyro was not - refined, similar to Phoebe in his manners and bearing. And they shared a past. Tyro could never offer her those things.

A moment comparing him to her fiancé in person had probably been enough to send her packing.

But what would happen to Atlas? Would Tyro be permitted to accompany them so he could guard the child, or would that wealthy Terran boy pull strings to get a different warrior.

The idea of losing the child shattered his heart.

Maybe Phoebe wouldn't tell the man about her relationship with Tyro. He had been kind to her, maybe she would do him that kindness in return, so that he could stay with Atlas.

But the idea of being near her, watching her marry another and bear his young...

Tyro took in deep breaths of the crisp evening air. He was not in control of what Phoebe decided to do. He was only in control of what he did. He had to focus on that.

He walked on for what felt like hours, trying to know what to do, and longing for the council of his brothers. Their advice had always helped him with difficult decisions in the past. But they were scattered across this moon, tending to their own charges. He only hoped their missions were going better than his own.

Finally, the scent of good food in the air had him heading toward the village. He hadn't eaten dinner. Food and drink might help him focus.

But before he made it to the door of the saloon, a familiar figure in a red dress came out, her pale tentacles glowing in the starlight.

"Saana?" he asked.

"You remembered," the friendly woman said with a smile. "Are you coming to the saloon for dinner? Where's your wife and that nice fat baby of yours?"

His heart twisted in his chest and he couldn't answer.

"Hey, are you okay, big guy?" she asked.

"I... I don't know," he admitted. "Remember when you told me you could sell me whatever I want?"

"I do," she said, nodding, with a concerned look.

"Would you be willing to sell me some... advice?" he asked. "I don't have many friends in this new place."

She blinked at him in surprise.

"What kind of advice?" she asked. "My area of expertise is kind of specific."

"Advice on women and relationships," he said quietly.

"Yeah, I think I can do that," she said, giving him a half smile. "But you have to buy me dinner."

"Of course," he said.

"Come on," she told him. "We'll eat in my room so we can talk in private. I'll just call down the order."

He followed her to the door on the side of the saloon.

Two more women in red gowns were leaning against the wall. One clutched a pipe between her ample lips, purple smoke coming out of her nose, as if she were a dragon. The other was reading on a palm projector.

"Hey, stranger," the one with the book said, glancing up dispassionately. "Looking to double your pleasure?"

"Or triple?" the one with the pipe offered, releasing a mouthful of fragrant smoke.

"I'm flying solo tonight, ladies," Saana said.

"Boo," said the one with the pipe. The other was already nose deep in her reading again.

Tyro followed Saana in the door and up a set of rickety stairs.

She took his hand and led him down a narrow hallway to the end, and then opened the door to reveal a small room.

Tyro wasn't sure what he had expected, but it wasn't this.

The space was neat and tidy with a small table and chairs, nicely made bed, and holo-paintings on the walls depicting gardens of different kinds from all over the system.

"It's lovely," he told her, striding up to one of the holos.

"That's the hanging garden of Welmurc," she told him, a fond expression on her face as she gazed at the painting, as if it were her child.

"You like gardens," he realized out loud as he looked around.

"I do," she said. "Feel free to look around while I order our meal."

He admired each of the holo paintings as she called the kitchen from her comm and ordered what sounded like a kingly meal.

It was fine. He could afford it, and he was feeling hollow inside. Even if he wasn't hungry, eating was probably a good idea.

"Sit," she offered, pointing to the bed.

He pulled out a chair at the little table instead.

"You really do just want to talk," she said, a bemused expression on her face. Her tentacles flowed as if she were standing in a brisk breeze.

"You are very beautiful," he told her. "But I have a mate bond to the woman you saw me with before."

"She's not your wife?" Saana asked.

"No," he said. "And I learned tonight that she has a fiancé already."

"Wow," Saana said, her tentacles falling flat next to her ears. "So tell me everything, I'm here to listen. And if I can help I will, but no promises."

But before he could begin, there was a knock at the door. The kitchen here worked fast.

Saana hopped up and helped the waiter droid lay out a huge meal and flagons of luxberry wine on the little table.

When they were finished Tyro paid and, thinking of Phoebe, gave the droid a nice tip.

It beeped and whirred excitedly as it rolled away.

"You tip droids?" Saana asked.

"Phoebe taught me to be kinder to them," he said, shrugging.

"I think that's really nice," Saana said.

He noticed her eyeing the table.

"Please, eat," he told her. "I'm not that hungry, so I'll talk to you while you enjoy your meal."

He watched as she piled food on her plate, placed a napkin in her lap and used a knife and fork to cut her food into tiny bites with incredible speed.

"I knew as soon as I met Phoebe that she was my mate," he said slowly. "That's the way of the dragons. If we are lucky enough to find a bond mate, we have no choice in the matter."

"So you wouldn't have chosen her otherwise?" Saana asked between bites.

"Not at first," he admitted. "She seemed so cold, so distant from everything around her."

"That could be cultural," Saana pointed out. "I deal with people from all over the system. Some of my most passionate clients are very restrained in their manner."

"Yes," Tyro said, smiling in recognition. "That's exactly it. As I got to know her, I could see that she is not detached at all. She's smart and energetic and resourceful."

Saana smiled and took a long sip of the gently glowing wine. He tried not to think of the image of Phoebe's face the first time she'd seen the berries glowing.

"She comes from wealth, I think," Tyro said. "So this life is challenging for her. But she's trying, I've seen her change her approach already. She's trying to be kind, to be patient."

"So not such a bad mate bond after all," Saana said.

"I'm grateful for the bond," he said. "I was eager to claim

her, and I thought she wanted me to take her too, though it hadn't happened yet."

"What are you waiting for?" Saana asked.

"I wanted her to understand what she was taking on," he said, feeling stupid. "So the first night, I wouldn't let myself give in and take her. I regret it, believe me. Then last night, someone showed up on our dock right before we could complete the claiming. And tonight, her fiancé appeared."

"That must have been awkward," Saana said sympathetically.

"It was infuriating," Tyro said. "She is mine and I am hers. How could she not tell me about him? And how could she not send word to him that she didn't want him any longer? What kind of woman is she?"

Saana frowned and then took a bite of her dinner instead of answering.

He watched her eat, wondering suddenly if she was bolting down her dinner because she didn't often get enough food to stem her hunger. Few people on this moon could afford a meal like the one they were sharing.

She cleaned her plate and then took another long pull of wine.

"Gods, but that was good," she said, wiping her mouth daintily with her napkin. "Thank you."

"My pleasure," he told her.

"Do you want my advice?" she asked.

"That's why I'm here," he said.

"You might not like it," she told him.

"Nonetheless."

"Wanting to claim your mate is all fine and well," she began. "But it's not fair for one person to impede another's freedom. That goes for her fiancé, and for you as well. She has a right to decide what's best for her. Your first instinct to hold off on claiming her was the right one."

"But she would have been mine," he said sadly.

"I have heard it said that if you love something, you should be able to let it go," she said. "If it comes back, it is yours, if it doesn't it never was."

"Those are wise words," he said, impressed.

"They came from some book Mootie was reading," she said dismissively.

"Is she the one from outside?" he asked.

"Yeah, that's her," Saana said. "Always has her face in a book, that one. You should eat something."

"I'm fine," he said, standing. "Share the rest with your friends if they aren't busy. I need to go now."

"Thanks," Saana said, her eyes shining at the bounty she'd been given.

His heart sank a little at the evidence that the workers weren't eating well.

He pulled out a stack of credits and laid them on the table.

"For your time," he said.

"No, no, that's okay," she said.

"I insist," he told her. "Your time has value."

He stalked out of the room and down the hall before she could argue.

"Thank you," she called to him. "She'd be a fool not to come back to you, you know."

He smiled as he headed down the stairs.

The two women leaning on the building ignored him but he waved good-bye to them anyway.

Early-morning light colored the sky pink as he hit the mostly-deserted street. The sounds and scents of the village waking up filled his senses.

The dragon in his chest moaned in sorrow for his mate and child.

Thinking of Saana and her friends being hungry made him want to provide for his own mate.

He decided to stop at one of the shops for provisions. Whatever happened, she would need to eat, and he didn't trust that snotty fiancé to provide for her here on a frontier moon.

He headed into the main grocer's market and gathered an armful of food that would be easy for her to prepare, even if she sent him away.

Another man was at the counter, covering it with fresh produce and cuts of meat. Something about him was familiar.

"Guckett?" Tyro said, barely recognizing the man they had caught sneaking onto their dock the night before last. He looked much better when he wasn't committing crimes while covered in lake-muck.

"Hey, there," the man said, turning with a genuine smile.

"You're stocking up," Tyro noticed aloud. "Your luck must have changed."

"I found gold on the beach," the man said, his eyes shining as he pulled a golden chain out of his pocket and held it out to the shopkeeper.

"Let me just weigh that," the man said, pulling out a laser scale.

"You just found that, on the beach?" Tyro asked.

"It's a miracle," the man replied, turning back to the shopkeeper who was holding out a huge stack of credits in change. "My idiot brother always said there was treasure in the lake from the lost settlement. Guess he was right after all. He's still an idiot, though.

"Let me help you carry this stuff out," Tyro offered.

"No need," the shopkeeper said. "My droids will assist you, sir. Please come again."

The man nodded with a delighted expression and watched the two droids load up his purchases.

"Will that be all?" the man asked Tyro.

"Sure, yes," Tyro said distractedly.

He made his purchase quickly and headed back past the beach to the docks of Phoebe's farm.

Down near the shoreline he could see people combing through the sand. Their neighbor must have shared news of his find with his friends.

Tyro sincerely doubted anyone would find another piece of jewelry on the beach. Even one piece of such value was an unusual thing to find on a frontier moon.

But as he passed there was a small commotion and he saw a woman lift her fist to the sky, an electrum chain dripping with emeralds hanging from it.

He didn't need a laser scale to know that would feed her family for a year.

20

PHOEBE

Phoebe paced the floor of the yurt, a fussy Atlas on her shoulder.

Maybe it was just the morning light, but Phoebe thought his green skin tone was a little more pale than before.

Was he getting sick? Or was Tyro's absence causing the little one's chameleon-like skin coloration to change?

"I can't believe he was out all night," she fumed out loud.

Atlas stopped sobbing to listen.

"He didn't even give me a chance to explain about Cash," she went on. "I mean he's supposed to care about me and support me, but he just went marching away."

Atlas began to whimper again, so she stopped talking and rubbed the place between his little shoulder blades that sometimes made him burp.

She hoped he settled down and felt better soon. She was frustrated with all the men in her life except Atlas.

"I'm going to raise you to be respectful," she whispered into his silky hair.

Cash had a lot of nerve just showing up at her doorstep. He could have sent comms ahead, like a normal person.

But I ran from him...

And her father could have come himself, if he missed her so much. Why would he send Cash here, like the only way he wanted to see his daughter return was on the other man's arm?

Does he love the farm more than he loves me?

She knew she was being dramatic. Most likely Cash had offered to come since her father was needed during the camellia harvest.

But it was her father she missed. It was her father who had loved her, raised her, listened to her, and earned the right to show up and ask her to change her mind - not Cash.

And Tyro...

What kind of *mate for life* turned his back the minute the going got tough?

The door knob rattled and Tyro strode in and placed a bag of groceries on the kitchen counter as if he'd left ten minutes ago to run errands.

"Where have you been?" Phoebe demanded.

He turned to her, his dark eyes solemn.

"Phoebe," he said, his voice caressing her name. "I've done a lot of thinking. It's not fair for one person to impede another person's freedom."

He stopped speaking and gazed at her significantly.

She stared right back at him, fuming mad, but unwilling to yell at him since baby Atlas had finally drifted off on her shoulder.

So this big green idiot thinks he can stay out all night and then tell me to back off and not impede his freedom when I want to know where he was?

She said an inward prayer of thanksgiving that they weren't mated yet.

No matter where in the universe she went, men all seemed to be the same. Every last one of them wanted freedom for himself, but expected to find Phoebe right where they left her when they were finished.

Well this one had underestimated her ability to resist his precious mate bond.

"We should work on the pump," Tyro said in a disappointed way, turning on his heel and heading back for the door.

"Fine," she said, following him.

She blinked against the brilliant sunlight reflecting off the lake.

"Good morning, madam," Saylin sang out as he rolled down the dock to her. "May I help with the little one so you can work?"

"Thank you," she said. "He's finally sleeping."

The droid extended his metallic arms and she placed Atlas gently between them.

"Thank you, Saylin," she said.

"It's my pleasure," the droid replied.

She noticed that he had begun playing Atlas's favorite color patterns on his front screen even though the little one was sleeping.

"He's lucky to have you," she murmured.

The droid buzzed and whirred with what she swore was pleased embarrassment as he rolled back toward the yurt with the sleepy baby.

"No," Tyro moaned from the far end of the dock.

Something was wrong.

She turned to see the green warrior on his hands and

knees, looking into the water, an expression of intense anguish on his face.

"What is it?" she asked, forgetting her anger and jogging up to join him.

He pointed at the water.

She knelt beside him and followed his gaze.

At first she thought the reflected light was making it too hard to see anything below the surface of the lake.

Then she realized what was going on.

The berries were gone. The fencing was gone.

Everything was gone.

This wasn't a missing impeller or a kinked hose. This was everything. The end of her farm. The end of her chance to make it on her own on this far-flung moon.

Phoebe rose to her feet, weightless as a ghost, and headed back down the dock.

"Where are you going?" Tyro demanded.

"Don't impede my freedom," she yelled back to him as she stalked away.

21

PHOEBE

Phoebe was face to face with the same equipment shop salesman she had negotiated with what felt like a lifetime ago.

She had been on top of the world then - flush with capital and resources, falling in love... She had been proud of her ability to strike a bargain.

Now she stood before him, humbled.

"It's gone," she said sadly. "It's all gone."

"Someone stole your *whole farm*?" the salesman asked dubiously.

"I don't want to believe it, but we've had other things stolen already," she said. "Maybe there's fencing with a built-in alarm system?"

"There is, but it has to be ordered in from off-moon, and the cost is prohibitive," he told her. "I'm guessing they took all your tools, too?"

"No, they didn't touch the tools," she said, shaking her head.

"You mean to tell me someone went to the trouble to

steal fencing and an unripened crop, but they left your valuable tools sitting there?" he asked.

"It doesn't make sense, I know," she said. "But someone ripped a hole in the fence the day before and we had to repair it. They didn't take anything then either. I think the point is to sabotage me, not necessarily to steal."

"Wait, wait, wait, you repaired the fence yesterday?" the salesman asked.

"Yes," she said. "But it doesn't matter now."

"What did you use for patching?" he asked.

"Some spare hose clamps and a crimping tool," she told him. "We had to improvise a bit."

The salesmen sucked in a breath through his teeth and shook his head.

"There's your problem," he explained. "Those clamps are meant to be used with the poly-synth hoses."

She didn't see what difference that would make. They weren't the ideal shape, but they had seemed plenty strong to hold the fencing in place.

"You see," he continued, clearly sensing that she did not see at all. "Poly-synth hoses are non-reactive. The metal in the clamps would start to deteriorate the second it came into contact with your fencing. If you have an electrified setup, the result would be ten times worse, especially without a really good circulation system."

It was like he was describing her *exact* setup.

"My God," she breathed. "I sabotaged my own farm."

"I'm so sorry," he told her sincerely.

"No, no," she said. "I'm grateful, actually. It broke my heart to think someone would do this. I'm glad it was just my own ignorance."

"If you need advice, just stop by anytime," he said kindly. "My name is Letz. I'm always glad to help."

"Thank you," she said.

"Do you still want to put together that special order?" he offered.

"I can't really afford it right now," she admitted. "Anyway, I'm not sure luxberry farming is really the life for me, after all. Do you buy used tools and equipment if I decide to pack it up?"

"Sure," he replied. "I'll be here when you figure it out. And I get it, luxberries are fussy. They require a lot of work and attention. But what an incredible thing to see them light up when your work is done."

She nodded to him over the lump in her throat.

All she could think about was the night she and Tyro had spent after she had seen the berries light up the water for the very first time.

She longed for her big green warrior, even though she was mad at him.

Phoebe headed out into the afternoon sunlight and started back toward the farm as she tried to decide what to do. She was so lost in thought that she nearly walked right into two women in scarlet gowns who were standing outside the saloon.

One had her nose buried in a palm projected novel. The other was puffing out lazy circles of purple smoke from a slender pipe.

"Oh, now she's here to get hers," the pipe smoker said in a husky voice.

"Pretty thing, don't let him have all the fun," the reader said, slipping her projector into her pocket and turning eagerly to Phoebe.

"What are you talking about?" Phoebe asked.

"Don't play coy," the smoker said. "We know you're here to get revenge for your husband spending last night with Saana. Wait until he hears you had both of us today."

"We'll give you a discount," the reader said conspiratorially.

"Tyro was here last night?" she asked.

"All night," the smoker said. "And he must have had the time of his life. He ordered enough food to feed us all and left Saana with a king's ransom to boot."

"Come on, pretty thing," the reader said, tugging at Phoebe's dress. "Let's even up the score."

"Um, no thank you," Phoebe managed, extricating herself from the woman's grip. "But thank you for telling me. I'm glad to know the truth."

Then someone called to her from the road that led back to her farm.

"Madam, madam," a man's voice shouted in a high-edged tone. "Come with me to the docks. Come quick."

Phoebe's heart dropped to her stomach.

All she could think was that something terrible must have happened to Tyro or Atlas.

She had turned and walked away for an hour, and something horrible had happened.

She ran for home as fast as she could, legs pumping and heart pounding, all thoughts of saloon women and farming forgotten.

My mate, my child... what have I done?

22

PHOEBE

Phoebe could see the crowd of people gathered around her dock as she sprinted toward home.

More than a few of them were moving around in the water.

Had someone drowned?

She was pretty sure Tyro couldn't drown.

Her feet pounded the deck, like distant drums in her addled brain.

As she got closer, she saw an older woman with a green baby in her arms.

Atlas.

She felt a sweet relief that even the fear of what might have happened to Tyro could not overshadow.

"Phoebe," a deep voice said from the water.

As one, the crowd turned in her direction.

Atlas squeaked and put his arms out to her.

Phoebe rushed over, and the woman smiled so hard her wrinkles disappeared as she handed him over.

"Wh-what's happening?" Phoebe asked, searching the water and finding Tyro's face.

He looked fine - happy really, rivulets dripping down his muscled form, a smile on his face.

"We know what you did, dear," the woman who had been holding Atlas told her in a voice that was too quiet for the others to overhear.

"What do you mean?" Phoebe asked, though she suspected she knew.

She noticed the people gathered around the dock comparing the sparkling jewels she had littered on the beach last night when she hoped no one was looking. They had found it much faster than she'd anticipated. She guessed that once word got out, everyone must have really started treasure hunting.

"This jewelry is obviously Terran," the woman whispered conspiratorially. "You might not know it, but they don't make stuff like that around here."

Phoebe felt her cheeks burning and she looked down at the dock. She couldn't even do anonymous kindness the right way.

"Please don't let any of them give any of it back," she murmured. "It was my mother's. I didn't earn it, and I don't wear it. I never even knew her. I only brought it to sell off in case of emergency. And the state of this lake is an emergency for all of us. I know everyone hates me. I just wanted to do some good."

"You asked my husband if you could help and he was too proud to accept," the woman said kindly. "So you found a way to help anyway. If you ask me, that makes you a good neighbor."

Phoebe felt hot tears prickle her eyes.

When the woman wrapped an arm around her, she allowed herself to be pulled into an embrace.

"Now, now," the woman said as Phoebe sobbed. "You've

been a wonderful neighbor to us, and we wanted to return the favor. So when you're done having a good cry, why don't you see what your husband and his new friends are up to?"

Phoebe straightened out of her own new friend's embrace and wiped her eyes with the arm that wasn't wrapped around Atlas.

"Come see, Phoebe." Tyro's deep voice was encouraging.

She moved to the edge of the dock and knelt to look into the water.

He was working with a group of men to replace their fence. The job was nearly finished, and the result was a sturdy-looking mishmash of different styles and colors of fencing.

"Everyone donated what they could spare from their own farm," Tyro said quietly.

"It's beautiful," she murmured, meaning it.

"I'm glad you came back," he said. "I tried to take Saana's advice, but setting you free because I love you was harder than I could have imagined."

"What?" she asked, genuinely confused.

"I spent the whole night at Saana's place," he told her. "She gave me advice about relationships."

"Look, you can at least be honest with me about what you did," she said. "We're not mated yet, so I'm willing to give you a pass. But you can *never* do that again if we're going to be together."

"What are you talking about?" he asked.

"The other women at the saloon told me you had so much fun you bought her a feast and left her with a small fortune," she said. "Where I come from that kind of thing is unacceptable if you're in a relationship."

"I fed her because she seemed hungry," he said, understanding dawning on his handsome features. "And I paid her for her time, since it's valuable. But I promise you, I never touched her."

She stared at him in awe.

He was telling the truth, she could feel it through the bond that sang between them, warm and sure.

"So when I asked you where you had been all night and you gave me that line about how it wasn't right for one person to impede another person's freedom..."

"I was talking about your freedom, Phoebe, not mine," he said, his eyes solemn. "My freedom was gone the moment you came into my sight. It belongs to you now."

"And you would have let me go with Cash?" she asked. "Just like that?"

"There was nothing *just like that* about it. It was the hardest thing I have ever had to do," he said plainly. "But I want you to be happy. No matter what it costs me."

"I know what will make me happy," she said.

"Then do it," he said. "And know that I will do whatever I can to support you, no matter what."

She took a deep breath and stood to face the gathered crowd.

23

TYRO

Tyro watched as Phoebe stood, her golden hair lifting slightly in the breeze, making her look like a goddess.

He had just set her free.

His beating heart was caught in her little hands.

He felt hopeless and relieved all at once.

"Neighbors," Phoebe called out in a passionate voice. "You have been so kind to us. Thank you for sharing your time, your hearts, and your materials with us."

A couple of people clapped and called their thanks back to her.

"I wonder if you can help with one more thing, and let me offer you something in return. I do not have the experience that you all clearly share when it comes to farming on this lake. But I can offer something else," she said. "I have access to some much-needed funding. And I want to use it to make life on this lake as good as possible, not just for me, but for all of us. The only problem is that I don't know what to do, or how to do it. I don't even know where to start. I was hoping that maybe we could all form a council so everyone can propose what to do and vote on how to spend the money. Is anyone willing to help?"

"We could buy better equipment and share it," one woman called out to her. "Then we'd all be able to farm more efficiently."

"We're all farming every year and it's impacting the water quality," a man said. "If we formed a co-op, we could each farm every other year and share the profits."

"Yes," another man called out. "We could plant sea-wort in the off-years to balance out the pH in the water."

"That could mean huge profits," the first woman said excitedly. "Big yields every other year for each of us and a beautiful lake all the time."

"We'd have more buying power too," another woman added. "And maybe we could even ship our excess crops off-moon and bring back more equipment if we pool for the cost of a freighter."

Tyro pulled himself out of the water and stood dripping on the dock, watching Phoebe's radiant smile as she took in all the excellent advice from her neighbors.

She was willing to give it all up - her farm back home, the fiancé who had traveled worlds to find her, the treasure she had smuggled here - all of it - just to offer their little family and the community around them a better life.

These neighbors, they were all as independent as she was - pioneers from distant planets. Each of them had been lured here by the promise of a way to work the land and water, and to bring happiness to their families, without answering to anyone else.

Yet with a simple act of kindness, and a humble plea for help, Phoebe had this disparate group eager to work together.

She was an incredible person.

Tyro wasn't sure he deserved her, but he was determined to do everything in his power to help her.

When Phoebe turned to him, her eyes filled with love and happiness, he felt his soul knit together with hers.

"Phoebe," he murmured helplessly.

She went to him, allowed him to fold her into his arms even though he was dripping with lake water.

"I love you, Phoebe," he whispered to her. "You are everything."

She went up on her toes and gazed into his eyes. "I love you too."

24

TYRO

Tyro stood at the end of the dock, watching the sunset turn the water fiery red.

Their neighbors, Agatta and Nesmarq, were going to take care of Atlas for a few days. They had all become fast friends after they began working together on ideas for the council and learned how much they had in common, including a little one of their own, just about the same age as Atlas. They'd been absolutely delighted at the idea of an extended playdate for the boys.

He watched his child get smaller and smaller, cradled in Agatta's strong arms, as Nesmarq rowed the boat to the next dock down from theirs.

Saylin sat on the boat as well, the large helper droid looking a bit out of place in the romantic scene. He had insisted on accompanying the neighbors in order to help with the baby.

But Tyro knew he was really performing his primary duty, keeping the youngling from harm.

And Tyro was grateful for it. He would rest easily, knowing that he'd be able to hear the droid's alarm if anything went wrong. The next dock over was barely a wing flap away for a dragon.

Not that he had much rest in mind. He was going to be tied up for the next few days.

The breeze carried the scent of Myrrish soap pearls from the yurt, and he nearly groaned with desire. Phoebe was in there now, bathing and preparing for him to claim her as his own.

The idea filled him with wild lust, even as he tried to temper it with restraint.

Just as he had been honest with her about Saana, she had been honest with him about Cash, who was probably halfway back to his home by now, with a renewed promise of a strictly business partnership from Phoebe and her family.

Phoebe was adamant that Cash had never so much as touched her, and neither had anyone else, not until Tyro.

Though the dragon in his chest was exultant at this news, Tyro himself felt the weight of responsibility of the task ahead of him. He was not merely claiming Phoebe tonight, he was initiating her into the world of sensuality.

By all the gods, he would make her love it, even if he died trying to hold back his own violent desire. He wanted her to crave him as much as he craved her.

Her shadowy figure appeared against the wall of the yurt, all curves and graceful movement.

It was time.

He took a deep breath of the crisp night air and headed for the door.

Time seemed to lose all meaning, the short walk down the dock stretching to an eternity.

He opened the door and she was waiting.

"Tyro," she murmured.

Her hair was damp and darker than usual, her scent too clean and fresh.

I will make you sweat and scream.

"Phoebe," he said as calmly as he could.

She moved to him so happily she practically floated, flowing into his arms and making him delirious with her warmth and softness.

He bent to kiss her, tasting her sweet lips chastely at first, then plundering her mouth when she sighed and pressed herself against him.

She whimpered a little and then pulled back as if surprised at herself.

"You need me, love," he told her gently. "We need each other."

She smiled up at him and his heart felt like it was burning in his chest.

He kissed her again, trying desperately to hold himself back.

But she slid her little hands under his shirt, as if hungering for his flesh against hers.

He helped her lift it off and peeled off his breeches too, stripping quickly until he stood before her naked as if he were her servant on a pleasure cruiser.

Her eyes were bright with lust as her gaze caressed his chest, abs, and down to rest on his cock, which throbbed helplessly for her, thick and proud.

Her mouth was parted slightly and he did not know if it was desire or fear that kept her eyes trained on him.

"My sweet mate," he said softly. "I will not take you until you are ready. Let me kiss you and love you. Do not be afraid. I will not claim you until you beg."

Her eyes snapped up to his and he watched as she slid her index finger down the clasp holding her robe.

The silky fabric slid down her body to pool on the floor at her feet, as if she were the statue of Venaed emerging from the pools of Ignis-7.

Tyro joined it on the floor, grasping her naked hips in his hands, and nuzzling the tender flesh of her inner thighs.

She gasped, but didn't pull away.

He pressed his mouth to her belly and nearly purred with satisfaction when her hands touched his shoulders, tentatively at first, then moved to tangle in his hair.

When he nuzzled her breasts, she whimpered again, nipples taut as if begging for his tongue.

He licked one into his mouth, loving the sounds she made.

He moved to the other and back again, going mad with her every cry.

When her hips began to tremble in his hands, he knew it was time.

He stood, towering over her once more.

"Bed," he heard himself say, in a voice that was thick with lust. "Now."

25

PHOEBE

Phoebe fell back on the bed, her whole body surging with desire.

She had never felt this way before, drunk with lust, so needy that the movement of the air in the room seemed to tease her heightened senses.

Tyro stood over her, his muscled body blocking out the lamplight.

She reached for him wordlessly, her soul aching for his.

He crawled onto the bed, his weight shifting her as if she were on a choppy sea. He stopped when he was between her legs, parting her with one big hand and then lowering his dark head to press his lips to her.

Phoebe cried out, lifting her hips to meet his mouth, shameless in her search for relief from the lust that held her in its thrall.

Tyro growled and latched his mouth onto her, licking and sucking, feeding on her as she moaned and begged.

Waves of pleasure lifted her, she was close, so close, her body taut and ready. But he pressed one last kiss to her, and kissed his way up her belly and breasts to cage her head in his arms.

She had been afraid of this moment, at least a little.

Now she was desperate to have him inside her.

"Phoebe, what do you want?" he growled.

"I want you," she moaned.

"Forever?" he asked.

"Yes, forever," she told him, gazing into his dark eyes.

"There will be pain," he warned her.

"I want it all," she gasped.

"Then you are mine," he told her.

She swore she heard the voice of the dragon in chorus with his. The sound sank into her bones, and she moaned with need for them both.

Tyro took himself in his hand, his jaw clenched, eyes burning.

She kept her eyes open, terrified that if she closed them, he would stop.

He pressed himself against her, his cock huge and throbbing, sending thrills through her. For a moment she wondered if it was even possible for her to take him in.

There was an instant of pinching pain as he pressed slowly inside her, stretching her until she gasped.

"Gods, Phoebe," he groaned, holding himself perfectly still, as if allowing her to accommodate herself to his girth.

And then the pain was gone, replaced by a sense of desperate urgency.

"Please," she whimpered, trying to lift her hips, though his weight pinned her down.

He roared and dragged himself out of her, sending her flying when he thrust into her again.

She clung to him, her body singing.

He thrust again, deep and slow.

Phoebe was delirious with the pleasure of it. She sank her nails into his arms, hips quivering.

"Mine," he groaned with each thrust. "*Mine, mine, mine.*"

The pleasure lifted her up and she was lost in it, desperate for the spark that would push her over the edge and end this torment.

"Please," she moaned.

His eyes went hazy with lust and he eased a hand between them, massaging her clitoris with a calloused thumb.

Phoebe hung on the air for a breathless moment and then the pleasure crashed down on her in waves.

She cried out, clinging to him as she felt him swell impossibly and then shout out his own pleasure as he jetted and pulsed inside her, sending her into a delirium of ecstasy that seemed almost endless.

At last, he collapsed on her chest.

She could hear her heart beating in her ears.

Or maybe that was his.

A hush seemed to have fallen over the lake, even the birds had stopped their cries. She closed her eyes, relishing this feeling of oneness with the man she loved.

"How do you feel, my mate?" he asked her, rolling over and pulling her onto his chest.

"Incredible," she whispered, smiling.

"It doesn't hurt?" he asked.

"It only hurt for a minute," she told him. "And then... oh, Tyro."

She would be overcome by that memory forever, she was sure of it.

He smiled at her, his gaze hooded.

"Do you need anything?" he asked.

"What do you mean?"

"Something to eat?" he offered. "A glass of water? We have to keep up our strength, and we only have a few minutes."

"Until what?" she asked.

But she felt it already, the inevitable pull that threatened to turn her inside out unless he claimed her again.

Her nails sank into his flesh as she pulled him back in.

"Yes," he groaned. "Yes, yes, yes."

26

PHOEBE

Phoebe stood at the crest of the hill where it all began, overlooking the frontier moon of Clotho from the exact spot where she'd first laid eyes on it.

The breeze ruffled her familiar lavender gown and lifted her hair as she let her gaze fall over the lush blue and green landscape. She took in the wooded crest, the small village, and the shimmering lake below.

Her hand went to the single camellia bloom she wore in her hair, to make sure it was still in place. She had almost given up on her struggling little plant until one of the neighbors had shown her the trick of planting it alongside a handful of local herbs that would help it maintain the conditions it needed to thrive.

And now, much like Phoebe herself, it seemed perfectly happy in its new home.

"Can you believe we're up here again?" Aurora asked from just behind her, snapping her out of her thoughts.

Phoebe turned to her friend, happy to hear the mischief in that contralto voice once more, and even more happy to see Aurora's fiery hair down and free. It was good to see that the Fox didn't have to hide anymore.

Luna, the third member of their little group of moon-moms, came into view.

"I get why we came up here for the wedding," Luna huffed, climbing up the hillside to join them. "But did we really have to resurrect these dumb gowns?"

The woman had all been wearing the eggplant-colored dresses when they arrived on Clotho, and they left very little to the imagination.

"I don't know about your mates, but Tyro really appreciates the cut of this thing," Phoebe laughed, glancing down at her plunging neckline. "Besides it's good luck for the three of us to match. And it's not like the general store sells wedding gowns. It was this or brown and yellow gingham. Believe me, I checked."

"Hey, if it's good enough for the sheriff, it's good enough for you two," Aurora said, giving them a monstrous wink.

She had recently been appointed interim sheriff, but the buzz around town was that she was a lock for the full-time gig.

"Where's your badge?" Luna asked Aurora.

"I can't believe you had to ask her that," Phoebe said. "You're just setting her up."

"Why?" Aurora asked innocently. "Where do you think it is?"

"Your garter," Phoebe said, rolling her eyes.

"Wrong," Aurora cried triumphantly, "it's in my *bra*. My *blaster* is in my garter."

Aurora lifted her gown so they could see a regulation sheriff's blaster tucked into the lace garter that encircled her thigh.

"Please tell Kade to be careful," Phoebe advised her, raising an eyebrow.

"Tell me to be careful about what?" Kade asked, his deep voice carrying on the breeze from somewhere farther down the hill.

"They're here," Luna squeaked, her hands going automatically to her hair and dress.

"You look amazing," Phoebe assured her.

The three grabbed each other's hands instinctively and Phoebe couldn't help remembering the last time they were up here, clinging to each other.

She had been so frightened.

And she had been so wrong about so many things.

The sound of singing rose to meet them from the hillside below.

"What the heck?" Aurora said.

This was supposed to be a very simple ceremony with just the three women, their mates, and the babies, presided over by the magistrate.

But as Phoebe stood, her eyes peeled for Tyro, she was greeted by the voices of dozens of friends and neighbors, humming the anthem of Clotho.

First Noxx appeared on the hillside, his hair dark and his eyes darker when he set his sights on his mate. Phoebe swore she could *feel* Luna blushing without even looking at her.

Kade arrived next, his green eyes lighting up when he saw his red-haired mate waiting for him.

At last Tyro joined his brothers at the crest.

He wore his full battle regalia, silver epaulets gleaming in the sunlight, leather crossing his bare chest, leaving thick muscles on full display.

They locked eyes and she could feel the electricity all over again.

The first few days after the claiming had been spent in full service to the thrall. Phoebe didn't remember eating or sleeping, though they must have done both of those things at some point.

Even a week later it was hard to accomplish simple tasks without surrendering to the dragon's need to mate.

They had managed to care for Atlas once the neighbors brought him home, and make a few plans for the first council meeting, but that was about it.

And now that she had spent an hour away from him, the thrall threatened to begin all over again.

She wasn't sure whether to be joyful or afraid.

"It gets easier," Luna whispered to her. "A little at least. Eventually…"

Her neighbors, Agatta and Nesmarq, arrived next on the crest, both of them singing for all they were worth. Agatta was cradling Atlas, and Nesmarq held an armful of fragrant flowers.

Slowly, the rest of the well-wishers arrived, various friends carrying baby Lyra, baby Sol and a dozen more bouquets of native flora.

The magistrate called Luna and Noxx forward and asked them to join hands. She spoke the words of the ceremony as she braided flowers around their forearms.

It was unlike any Terran wedding Phoebe had ever attended, but the idea was the same. They were standing under the sky, asking the heavens and their friends to guide them in caring for each other.

Compared to a mating bond, it was probably just a silly formality. But it meant the world to Phoebe and her friends.

She watched as Noxx devoured Luna's mouth with a passionate kiss.

Then Aurora and Kade went forward to say their words and have their arms bound together with flowers.

Aurora's blue eyes were suddenly filled with tears when it was time for the kiss, and Phoebe felt her own eyes filling in sympathy.

This was such a happy moment for all of them.

The next thing she knew, Tyro was offering her his arm.

"Don't be frightened," he purred as they moved forward.

She wanted to tell him she wasn't afraid, that she was happy, so happy.

But when she opened her mouth there was a lump in her throat too big to speak over, and a tear slipped down her cheek.

"Phoebe," he breathed, stopping to take her by the shoulders. "Phoebe what's wrong? Have you…have you changed your mind?"

She shook her head, smiling through the tears. "The opposite," she managed. "I'm… I'm…"

"What is it?" he asked.

"I'm so happy," she sobbed.

He pulled her tight to his chest and she closed her eyes and breathed in the scent of leather and man, and the cooler, stranger hint of the dragon within.

"Shall we get married now?" he whispered into her hair.

"Yes," she said. "But hurry."

Desire was unfurling in her belly as if it would fly away with her.

We cannot tear each other's clothes off in front of all our friends and neighbors, she reminded herself.

But the temptation was real.

Tyro squeezed her hand and led her to the magistrate.

Time seemed to stand still as the flowers bound them together, and the words were spoken.

At last they were released and Tyro was wrapping her up in his arms.

There was so much she wanted to tell him, so much she wanted to thank him for. This mate of hers had given her the space and faith to let go of old fears, and to step up to be herself, separate from her land and her possessions.

He had fully supported her when she made a plan, and then sent Cash home with word to her father that he should work out a water deal that gave Cash's family right-of-first refusal if the camellia farm was ever sold.

She knew Tyro would back her play, no matter what.

Phoebe and Tyro and Atlas were happy right where they were. They could spend their off-years visiting her father on Terra 212, or he could come to them and learn all about submerged farming.

But Phoebe's life wasn't tied up in that land anymore.

It was tied up in her family.

And that was just the way she wanted it.

As Tyro's lips crashed down on hers, the sizzle between them still new, yet somehow as old as time, she knew she didn't need to say the words.

He understood.

He always would.

***

Thanks for reading Tyro!

Are you ready for another set of romantic adventures featuring a new trio of adorable babies from the Alien Adoption Agency on the brand-new moon of Lachesis?

Then make sure you preorder Zane and Sarah's story right away, so you don't miss a beat!

https://www.tashablack.com/alienadoption.html

And while you're waiting, how about some more steamy, intergalactic action that you can sink your teeth into RIGHT NOW?

Do you want to read about a space-pirate-in-training on her first solo mission to plunder an abandoned luxury cruiser, who assumes she'll be all alone aboard the big, empty ship, but is surprised to find a sinfully sexy alien who eyes her with a hunger that speaks of centuries of longing?

Then keep reading for a sample of Tolstoy: Stargazer Alien Barbarian Brides #1.
Or grab your copy now:
www.tashablack.com/sabb

TOLSTOY (SAMPLE)

1

ANNA

In a forgotten corner of the galaxy, far from the established trade routes, and even farther from where it was supposed to be, floated a long-forgotten ship, one among many.

And at the center of that abandoned ship grew a forest.

Anna Nilsson froze in place, wishing there were someone to share the unusual sight with her. But she was alone, the only sound the hiss of the air pump in her spacesuit.

She stepped closer, mesmerized.

After the endless burnished aluminum of the *Stargazer*, the lush greenery before her almost hurt to look at.

Anna stood in a derelict luxury star cruiser the size of a shopping mall. She'd already made her way through winding corridors of threadbare rugs and corroded, flickering chandeliers, using her tagger to mark items of interest along the way. The passageways circled rings of rooms that extended along the sides of the ship as far as she could see. She almost felt as if she were in a *Scooby Doo* episode, or visiting the sunken Titanic, until she opened the latest door.

Maybe it was the lack of sleep since she'd found out she would be running her first salvage mission completely solo, or maybe the oxygen mix in her suit was a little high, but Anna couldn't shake the feeling she'd stepped into a dream. She blinked to clear her head, but nothing changed.

She stood before a huge wall of glass, or something like glass, anyway. Beyond the wall, trees - real, honest to god trees - stretched upward, their lumpy branches bristling with bright green leaves. They had to be hundreds of years old.

As a child, Anna had visited the indoor rain forest exhibit at the Baltimore Aquarium on Earth. Clutching her big brother's hand, she'd dashed up the wooden platforms, trying to catch a glimpse of the sloth or the toucan. The trees there had been spread out, the bustling city always looming just outside the floor-to-ceiling windows.

What stood before her now was not an engineered approximation. It was a real forest, branches growing thick enough to block out the light source above. The surreal scene was made complete by a pair of ancient looking lamp posts glowing faintly at the edge of the tree line, their light barely penetrating a few steps into the wooded area.

The ship was as good as dead, but the forest was very much alive. Tendrils of ivy burst through the crevices between the corroded metal panels that held the glass in place, refusing to bend to the will of the man-made structure.

Hot tears sprung to her eyes and Anna had to lean over and rest her hands on her knees to steady herself in the wake of sudden emotion.

She hadn't seen a tree in six months.

Well, technically it had been far, far longer. But she tried not to think about that part.

Light from above filtered down into the woods, dappling the soil and stones beneath the trees.

For a moment Anna was back at the cafe in Tarker's Hollow, gazing out the window at the park as her mother scolded her to bus the lunch tables. She could smell the almond croissants baking, hear the mindless chatter of the patrons as they discussed whatever it was people with real lives discussed. It had been her entire existence, and now it was just... gone.

A light breeze sent a shiver of motion through the leaves in front of her. It must have been manufactured weather, still operating on reserve energy. The movement highlighted what she hadn't noticed before.

The plant life had run riot, but there were no birds, no squirrels, not even insects on the forest floor. Besides Anna, the forest was the only living thing on the ship.

She stepped closer, placed her gloved hand against the nearest pane in solidarity, and holstered her tagger. She couldn't imagine needing it in here.

A tremendous sycamore towered over her head just inside the glass.

She gazed up into its branches. The light seemed to be brightening above.

No. That wasn't right.

The tree was brightening.

Before her eyes, the green leaves faded then burst into flaming orange.

All around the sycamore the other trees erupted into a symphony of yellow, peach, pink and scarlet.

Anna was watching summer turn to fall, as if someone had pressed a button on the remote that controlled the speed of the world.

A tone sounded in her helmet.

She looked down at her wrist.

Her origami drone unfolded from its dock and then refolded itself into something resembling a bird, before fluttering up to her.

"The atmosphere is breathable," BFF19 sang out.

Anna released her helmet and pulled it off.

2
LEO

Leo watched from the shadows, his pulse racing.

The whole ship had been sleeping.

He had awoken hours ago, alone, with no memory of what happened.

Now the ship was waking too.

And he knew why.

They had a guest.

He crept closer, sticking to the shadows so as to avoid its notice, and watched as the strange creature placed an appendage against the glass wall of the forest.

It was covered from head to toe in suit and helmet, but it was bipedal and it moved in much the same manner as the former residents of the ship.

Something detached itself from the visitor's wrist, folded itself into a bird-like shape and hovered near its head.

A moment later, the creature unlatched its helmet and lifted it off.

It was female.

She shook out a curtain of flame colored hair, brighter

than the blush of the changing trees in the forest between them.

He had just enough time to take in her expression, tender, wondrous, maybe just a little lonely.

Then something stirred in Leo's chest and hot lust washed over him. His skin prickled, ready to change for her, to join her.

It seemed impossible. But he knew it to his bones.

This was the call of his blood mate.

Stronger than the strongest will, more ancient than the stars, the grip of his blood mate held him in her thrall. He gasped for breath, his eyes trained on the hall that separated them, searching for the fastest way to get to her.

Before he could decide, another zap of awareness electrified him.

Darkness pulled at him this time, incinerating him from within with pulsing red anger. He struggled against it, but the world went scarlet behind his eyes and the Other took over.

***

Thanks for reading this sample of Tolstoy!
Are you ready to see what happens when Anna and Leo uncover a baby who just might be the priceless clone of a famous cultural icon, then realize they must work together if they want to get out alive?

Then grab the rest of the story now!
www.tashablack.com/sabb

And don't forget to preorder the next book from the Alien Adoption Agency!

https://www.tashablack.com/alienadoption.html

TASHA BLACK STARTER LIBRARY

Packed with steamy shifters, mischievous magic, billionaire superheroes, and plenty of HEAT, the Tasha Black Starter Library is the perfect way to dive into Tasha's unique brand of Romance with Bite!
Get your FREE books now at tashablack.com!

ABOUT THE AUTHOR

Tasha Black lives in a big old Victorian in a tiny college town. She loves reading anything she can get her hands on, writing paranormal romance, and sipping pumpkin spice lattes.

Get all the latest info, and claim your FREE Tasha Black Starter Library at www.TashaBlack.com

Plus you'll get the chance for sneak peeks of upcoming titles and other cool stuff!

Keep in touch...
www.tashablack.com
authortashablack@gmail.com

facebook.com/romancewithbite
twitter.com/romancewithbite

Printed in Great Britain
by Amazon